THE
$\mathcal{S}$TRANGER
NEXT DOOR

Amélie Nothomb

Translated by Carol Volk

· THE ·

Stranger

NEXT DOOR

• • •

A NOVEL

ORIGINALLY PUBLISHED AS
Les Catilinaires

HENRY HOLT AND COMPANY
NEW YORK

Henry Holt and Company, Inc.
Publishers since 1866
115 West 18th Street
New York, New York 10011

Henry Holt® is a registered trademark of
Henry Holt and Company, Inc.

First published in the United States in 1998 by
Henry Holt and Company, Inc.
Published in Canada by Fitzhenry & Whiteside Ltd.,
195 Allstate Parkway, Markham, Ontario L3R 4T8.
Originally published in France in 1995 by
Albin Michel under the title *Les Catilinaires*

LIBRARY OF CONGRESS CATALOGING-IN-PUBLICATION DATA

Nothomb, Amélie.
[Catilinaires. English]
The stranger next door : a novel (originally published as Les
catilinaires) / Amélie Nothomb ; translated by Carol Volk.
p.   cm.
ISBN 0-8050-4841-3
I. Volk, Carol.   II. Title.
PQ2674.0778C3713   1998
843'.914—dc21   97-24566

First American Edition 1998

Designed by Kathryn Parise

Printed in the United States of America
All first editions are printed on acid-free paper.∞

1   3   5   7   9   10   8   6   4   2

Je te nommerai guerre et je prendrai sur toi les
libertés de la guerre et j'aurai entre les mains
ton visage obscur et traversé. . . .

I will name you war and I will take
With you the liberties of war, and I will have
In my hands your dark-crossed face. . . .

—Yves Bonnefoy,
"Vrai nom,"
translated by Galway Kinnell

THE
$\mathcal{S}$TRANGER
NEXT DOOR

$\mathcal{W}$e know nothing about ourselves. We think we're used to being ourselves, but it's just the opposite. The more the years pass, the less we understand the person in whose name we say and do things.

This is not a problem. What's wrong with living the life of a stranger? Maybe it's better that way: know yourself, and it will make you ill.

This ordinary estrangement wouldn't have bothered me if not for . . . How shall I put it? . . . If I hadn't met Mr. Bernardin.

I wonder when this story began. It's like the Hundred Years War: dozens of dates would be appropriate. It would be accurate to say that the affair began a year ago; it would also be accurate to say that it took shape six months ago. However, it would be more appropriate to situate its beginning around the time of my marriage, forty-three years ago. But the real truth, in the strongest sense of the word, is that the story began at my birth, sixty-six years ago.

I'll stick with the first option: it all began a year ago.

.   .   .

Some houses give orders. They are more domineering than fate: one look and you're defeated. You have to live there.

As my sixty-fifth birthday approached, Juliette and I were looking for a place in the country. We saw this house, and instantly we knew that it would be the house. Despite my distaste for capital letters, I feel compelled to write the House, for it would be the one we would never leave, the one that had been waiting for us, the one we had always been waiting for.

Always, yes: ever since Juliette and I have been husband and wife. Legally, it's been forty-three years. In reality, we have been married for sixty years. We were in the same class in kindergarten. We saw one another the first day of school and fell in love. We have never been apart since.

Juliette has always been my wife; she has always been my sister and my daughter as well—even though we're only a month apart in age. That's why we didn't have a child. I've never needed anyone else: Juliette is everything to me.

I was a high school teacher of Latin and Greek. I loved

my work and got along well with my few students.
Nonetheless, I awaited retirement as the mystic awaits
death.

My comparison is not gratuitous. Juliette and I have always aspired to be liberated from what men have made of
life. School, work, social events, even in their simplest
forms, were too much for us. Even our marriage ultimately
felt like a formality.

Juliette and I wanted to turn sixty-five, we wanted to
leave behind the world, which we considered to be a waste
of time. Though city dwellers from birth, we wanted to live
in the country, less out of a love of nature than out of a need
for solitude—a raging sensation akin to hunger, thirst, and
disgust.

When we saw the House, we had a wonderful feeling of
relief: this place we'd been aspiring to since childhood ex-
isted after all. If we had dared to imagine it, we would have
imagined a clearing just like this one, near a river, with this
house—the House—pretty, invisible, a wisteria climbing its
walls.

Four miles away was Mauves, the village, where we
could find everything we needed. On the other side of the
river was another, indiscernible house. The owner told us
that it was inhabited by a doctor. Had we needed reassur-
ance, this was even better: Juliette and I would be retiring

from the world, but thirty yards from our refuge would be a doctor!

We didn't hesitate an instant. In one hour, the house became the House. It wasn't expensive, there was no work to be done. There seemed to us no question that luck had held the reins in this affair.

.   .   .

It's snowing. When we moved here one year ago, it was also snowing. We were thrilled: from the first evening, these inches of whiteness gave us a strong impression of being at home. The next morning, we felt cozier than at any time during the previous forty-three years in our city apartment—an apartment from which we had nonetheless never moved.

Finally I could devote myself entirely to Juliette.

It's hard to explain: I've never felt I had enough time for my wife. In sixty years, what have I given her? She is everything to me. She says the same about me, yet it doesn't erase my deep-seated feeling of insufficiency. It's not that I consider myself bad or mediocre, but Juliette has never had anything or anyone but me. I was and am her life. This thought brings a lump to my throat.

What did we do those first days at the House? Nothing, I think, except for a few walks in the woods, so white and silent that we often stopped to stare at one another in amazement.

Aside from that, nothing. We had come to the place of our dreams. If our peace had not been disturbed, I know we would have lived that way until death.

This last sentence sends a chill down my spine, and I realize that I am telling the story all wrong. I am making mistakes—it's not that I'm being inexact or lying, but I'm making mistakes. It's probably because I don't understand the story myself: something about it escapes me.

One detail I remember perfectly from that first week is this: I was preparing a fire in the chimney, and naturally I was bungling it. It seems it takes years to achieve this feat. I had put together something that burned; it couldn't be called a fire, however, because it was clear it wouldn't last. Let's just say that I had caused a momentary combustion. I was proud at least of that.

Crouching by the fireplace, I turned my head and saw Juliette. She was seated in a low armchair next to me, and was contemplating the fire with that skeptical look she has of respectful concentration, the object of which, in this case, was our pitiful hearth.

I was startled: she hadn't changed a bit—not just since our marriage, but since our first encounter. She had grown a little taller—very little—her hair had whitened, but all the rest, which is to say everything, was the same to a stunning degree.

This gaze she fixed on the fire was the same as the gaze she had riveted on the teacher, at school. These hands resting on her knees, this motionless head, these calm lips, this well-behaved air of a child intrigued by the world around her—all were the same. I had always known she hadn't changed, but I had never realized to what degree.

This revelation filled me with emotion. I was no longer watching the precarious flame, I had eyes only for the little six-year-old girl with whom I had lived for nearly sixty years.

I don't know how many minutes it lasted. Suddenly, she turned her heard toward me and saw that I was watching her.

"The fire isn't burning," she murmured.

"Time doesn't exist," I said, as if that were an answer.

I had never been so happy in my life.

.   .   .

After one week in the House, we were convinced we had never lived anywhere else.

One morning, we took the car to the village to buy groceries. The store in Mauves was a delight to us: it didn't sell much, and this absence of choice made us inexplicably joyful.

On the way home, I observed, "Look, the neighbor's

chimney isn't smoking. It's possible to live here a long time and still not be able to make a fire."

Juliette couldn't get over having a garage: we had never had one before. As I was closing the door, she said:

"This house is the House for the car as well."

I understood the capital letter. I smiled.

We put our groceries away. The snow was beginning to fall again. My wife remarked that we had done well to do our shopping in the morning. Soon the road would be impassable.

This idea made me happy—everything made me happy. I said, "My favorite proverb has always been: 'To live happy, live hidden.' We're there, aren't we?"

"Yes, we're there."

"I can't remember which writer added, not long ago: 'To live hidden, live happy.' This is even truer. And it suits us even better."

Juliette was watching the snow fall. I could only see her back, but I knew how her eyes looked.

. . .

That same afternoon, at about four o'clock, someone knocked on the door.

I went to open it. It was a fat man who seemed older than I was.

"I'm Mr. Bernardin. Your neighbor."

9

What could be more normal than a neighbor coming to make the acquaintance of new arrivals, particularly in a clearing consisting of two houses? His face, moreover, could not have been more ordinary. I remember, nonetheless, standing there frozen, confused, like Robinson upon his first encounter with Friday.

Several long seconds ensued before I became aware of my rudeness and spoke the anticipated words:

"Of course. You're the doctor. Come in."

When he was inside the living room, I went to get Juliette. She looked frightened. I smiled.

"It's just a little courtesy call," I whispered.

Mr. Bernardin shook my wife's hand and sat down. He accepted a cup of coffee. I asked him if he had been living in the house next door for long.

"Forty years," he responded.

"Forty years here!" I said, in rapture. "How happy you must have been!"

He said nothing. I concluded that he had not been happy. I didn't press the matter.

"Are you the only doctor in Mauves?"

"Yes."

"Quite a responsibility!"

"No. No one is sick."

Nothing surprising about that. The population of the

village must not have been more than a hundred. What was the chance, then, of finding a person in ill health?

I tore some other basic information out of him—*tore* is the right word: he responded as little as possible. When I said nothing, he said nothing. I learned that he was married, that he had no children, and that in case of an illness, we could call on him. Which prompted me to say, "What a godsend to have you for a neighbor!"

He remained silent. He reminded me of a depressed buddha. At least you couldn't fault him for being a chatter-box.

For two hours, motionless in his chair, he responded to my innocuous questions. It took him a while to speak, as if he had to think, even when I was asking him about the weather.

There was something touching about him: I didn't doubt for an instant that he was bored by this visit. It was clear that he felt obliged to pay it by some naïve idea of decorum. He seemed to be desperately awaiting the moment when he could leave. I could see that he was too stiff and awkward to dare to speak the liberating words: "I won't bother you any longer," or, "Pleased to meet you."

After these two pathetic hours, he finally rose. I thought I could read this message of distress on his face: "I don't know what to say to leave without being rude."

Touched, I flew to his rescue:

"How nice of you to have kept us company! But your wife must be worried by your absence."

Without responding, he put on his coat, said good-bye, and left.

I watched as he walked away, stifling my desire to laugh. When he was already some distance, I said to Juliette, "Poor Mr. Bernardin! How heavily his courtesy call weighed on him!"

"He doesn't have much to say."

"Lucky for us! There's one neighbor who won't disturb us."

I held my wife in my arms and whispered, "Do you realize how alone we are here? Do you realize how alone we're going to be?"

It was all we had ever wanted, a happiness that cannot be named.

As the poet quoted by Scutenaire said, "We are never nothing enough."

.   .   .

The next day, at about four o'clock, Mr. Bernardin knocked on the door.

As I ushered him in, I imagined he would announce the courtesy call of Mrs. Bernardin.

The doctor took the same chair as the day before, accepted a cup of coffee, and sat silently.

"How have you been since yesterday?"

"Fine."

"Will your wife also pay us the honor of a visit?"

"No."

"She's well, I hope?"

"Yes."

"Naturally. The wife of a doctor couldn't possibly be in ill health, isn't that so?"

"No."

I pondered this for a moment, thinking of the logical rule of response. I was stupid enough to follow up with, "If you were Japanese or a computer, I would be forced to conclude that your wife is sick."

Silence. A bolt of shame flashed over me.

"Excuse me. I was a Latin teacher for nearly forty years, and sometimes I imagine that people share my linguistic obsessions."

Silence. It seemed Mr. Bernardin was looking out the window.

"It's not snowing anymore, fortunately. Did you see how much fell last night?"

"Yes."

"Does it snow this much here every winter?"

"No."

"Does the road get blocked by the snow sometimes?"

"Sometimes."

"Does it stay that way long?"

"No."

"Aha. The roads department takes care of it quickly?"

"Yes."

"That's good."

If, at my age, I remember with such precision a conversation that took place a year ago and was this insignificant, it's because of the slowness of the doctor's responses. To each of the aforementioned questions, it took him fifteen seconds to react.

This was to be expected, after all, on the part of a man who seemed about seventy years old. I considered that, in five years' time, I would perhaps be like him.

Timidly, Juliette sat down next to Mr. Bernardin. She was contemplating him with the look I have already described, full of respectful attention. His eyes remained unfocused.

"Another cup of coffee, sir?" she asked.

He refused with a "No." I was a bit shocked by the absence of a "thank you" or a "ma'am." It was clear that the words yes and no constituted the bulk of his vocabulary. And I was beginning to wonder why he was overstaying his welcome. He was saying nothing and had nothing to say. A suspicion sneaked into my mind:

"Is your heat working all right at home, sir?"

"Yes."

My experimental turn of mind prompted me nonetheless

to prolong the examination, a matter of exploring the limits of his concision.

"You don't have a fireplace, do you?"

"No."

"You have gas heat?"

"Yes."

"Does it cause you any trouble?"

"No."

This wasn't working. I ventured a question to which it was impossible to answer yes or no: "How do you spend your days?"

Silence. His face turned angry. He puckered his lips, as if I had offended him. This silent discontent affected me so much I began to feel ashamed.

"I'm sorry, that was nosy of me."

A second later, this retreat struck me as ridiculous. There was nothing indiscreet about my question! He was the one who was impolite, invading our home when he had nothing to say.

When I thought about it, I realized that even if he were talkative, his behavior would be rude. And would I have preferred that he drown me in a torrent of words? It's hard to say. But his silence was so enervating!

Suddenly I thought of another possibility: he had a favor to ask, but he didn't dare. I threw out various suggestions:

"Do you have a telephone?"

"Yes."

"A radio, a television?"

"No."

"Neither do we. You can live very well without them, can't you?"

"Yes."

"Are you having any car troubles?"

"No."

"Do you like to read?"

"No."

At least he was honest. But how could anyone live in this out-of-the-way place without a taste for reading? I was horrified. Particularly since he had said, the day before, that he didn't have any patients in the village.

"It's a nice place for strolling. Do you take many walks?"

"No."

I should have known, I thought, examining his fleshy body. Strange that a doctor would be so fat! I said to myself.

"Do you have a specialty?"

I obtained a response of record length.

"Yes, cardiology. But I practice as a generalist."

I was stupefied. This man who seemed like an idiot was a cardiologist. That meant years of difficult, strenuous studies. There was some intelligence in that head after all.

Fascinated, I reversed everything I had believed: my

neighbor had a superior mind. He took fifteen seconds to find answers to my simplistic questions as a way of emphasizing the stupidity of my inquiries. He didn't talk because he wasn't afraid of silence. He didn't read for some Mallarméan reason, in keeping with what I glimpsed in his sad flesh. His brevity and his predilection for yeses and nos made him a disciple of Saint Matthew and of Bernanos. His eyes that looked at nothing betrayed his existential dissatisfaction.

I decided to be silent too.

It was the first time in my life that I sat silently one-on-one with someone. To be more precise, I had done so with Juliette, but for us it was a form of communication. In the years since we were six years old, we had had the time to surpass language, but I couldn't hope for as much with Mr. Bernardin.

Yet at first I entered into his silence confidently. It seemed easy. All I had to do was stop moving my lips, stop looking for the next sentence. Alas, not all silences are the same: Juliette's was a padded universe, rich in promise and fantastical creatures, whereas the doctor's made you clench, left you feeling like a piece of measly flesh.

I tried to hold up longer, like a diver attempting to hold his breath. It was a frightful sojourn, the silence of our neighbor. My hands became damp and my tongue dry.

The worst of it was that our guest seemed annoyed by my experiment. He began looking at me with an outraged expression, as if to say, "How rude of you not to make conversation with me!"

I caved in. My fainthearted lips went into motion to produce a sound—any sound. To my great surprise, it was:

"My wife's name is Juliette, and mine, Emile."

I couldn't get over it. How ridiculous to be so friendly! I had never wanted to inform this gentleman of our first names. Why the devil had my phonatory mechanism behaved this way?

The doctor seemed to share my disapproval, for he didn't say anything, not even "Oh." Neither was there that vague echo in his eyes that could be translated as "I see."

I felt as if he had just crushed me in an arm-wrestling match. His face bore the coolness of triumph.

And I, the wretched loser, got myself in even deeper:

"And what is your name, sir?"

After the ritual fifteen seconds, his atonal voice responded, "Palamedes."

"Palamedes? Palamedes! How wonderful! Are you aware that Palamedes is the one who invented the game of dice, during the siege of Troy?"

I will never know if Mr. Bernardin was aware of this, for he said nothing. As for me, I was thrilled with this onomastic diversion.

"Palamedes! That fits with your Mallarméan side: 'A throw of the dice will never abolish chance!'"

Our neighbor seemed to accept my remark indulgently. He was silent, as if I had surpassed the limits of the absurd.

"Don't misunderstand me: I'm laughing because your name is unusual. But it's very pretty, Palamedes."

Silence.

"Was your father a teacher of ancient languages like mine?"

"No."

"No": that was all I had the right to know on the subject of Mr. Bernardin's father. I was beginning to find the situation irritating. I have always hated asking people questions. Ultimately that was why I had come to bury myself in this remote outpost. An outside observer might have considered the doctor to be in the right: first because I was being indiscreet, second because wisdom is never on the side of the one who is speaking. But this observer would be overlooking the fact that made this tête-à-tête incomprehensible, namely that this fellow was the one who was intruding in my home.

I was a hairbreadth from asking him, "Why did you come here?" The phrase wouldn't come out. It seemed too harsh; it could only be construed as a cue to leave. It's true that was what I wanted, but I didn't have the courage to be rude.

Palamedes Bernardin, however, possessed that courage: he sat there gazing at nothing, with a look at once idiotic and discontented. Was he aware how rude he was being? How could anyone tell?

In the meantime, Juliette remained seated next to him. She seemed to be finding him quite interesting, like a zoologist studying the behavior of a strange animal.

There was something comical about the contrast between her delicate frame, with her lively eyes, and the inert mass of our neighbor. Unfortunately, I didn't feel I had the right to laugh. For the first time in my life, I regretted my polite education.

What the devil else could I say to him? I scratched my head in search of an innocuous subject.

"Do you ever go to the city?"

"No."

"You find everything you need in town?"

"Yes."

"There isn't much, though, at the grocery store in Mauves."

"Yes."

"Yes." Yes? What did this yes mean? Wouldn't a no have been more appropriate? The linguistic itch was creeping back when Juliette intervened:

"There wasn't any lettuce there, sir. Of course, it's not the season, but it's hard to live without lettuce. Is there any in spring?"

The question seemed to surpass the intellectual capacity of our guest. After believing he was a wise man, I returned to the first hypothesis: he was a retard. Because if he wasn't an idiot, he would have responded either "yes," "no," or "I don't know."

Again he looked annoyed. Yet no one could call my wife's words indiscreet. I stepped in with exaggerated respectfulness:

"Come now, Juliette, does one ask a man such as Mr. Bernardin household questions?"

"Doesn't Mr. Bernardin eat salad?"

"That's Mrs. Bernardin's business."

She turned back to the doctor to ask this question, whether sincerely or impertinently I wasn't sure:

"Does Mrs. Bernardin eat salad?"

I was on the verge of intervening when, after his usual period of reflection, he said, "Yes."

The simple fact that he deigned to respond proved that the question was a good choice. This must be the kind of thing one could ask him. With a list of vegetables, we could make out for some time.

"Do you eat tomatoes as well?"

"Yes."

"Turnips?"

"Yes."

The catalog of vegetables was a marvelous solution, but

a certain sense of decency prevented me from continuing. Too bad, because it was getting to be fun.

I remember floundering for a long while between periods of silence and inept inquiries.

At about six o'clock he rose to leave as he had the day before. I had lost all hope. I can't express how interminable these two hours had seemed to me. I was exhausted, as if I had just fought the cyclops—or worse, its opposite. Indeed, the cyclops was called Polyphemus, or "the one who talks a lot." Confronting a chatterbox is an ordeal, no doubt about it, but what can you do with someone who invades your home to impose his silence?

The day before, I had laughed after the neighbor left. That day, I wasn't laughing anymore. Juliette asked me, as if I were omniscient, "Why did he come today?"

To comfort her, or perhaps myself, I invented this implausible response:

"Some people think that one courtesy call isn't enough, that you have to pay two. Now we're off the hook."

"Ah! It's just as well. That fellow takes up a lot of space."

I smiled. Yet I was fearing the worst.

· · ·

The next morning, I woke up nervous. I didn't dare admit the reason, and to escape my vague anxiety, I developed a real country project.

"Let's make ourselves a Christmas tree today."

Juliette was dumbfounded.

"But Christmas is over. It's January."

"So what?"

"We've never had a Christmas tree!"

"This year, we'll have one."

Like a general, I organized the operations: we would go to the village to buy the tree and the decorations. In the afternoon, we would install the tree in the living room and decorate it.

It goes without saying that I didn't care whether I had a Christmas tree or not. It was all I could think of to quell my unease.

In the village, there were no more Christmas trees for sale. We bought a few garlands and colored balls, as well an ax and a saw. On the way home, I stopped the car in the middle of the forest and, with the clumsiness of a neophyte, cut down a small pine tree. I placed it in the trunk, which I had to leave open.

In the afternoon, we went to great lengths to get the tree to stand erect in the living room. I decided that the following year, we would take one with its roots and put it in a pot. Next, we distributed the decorations, which were of questionable taste, over the branches. My wife was having lots of fun: she found the tree to be as smart as a village woman leaving the hairdresser. She suggested adding a few curlers.

Juliette seemed to have forgotten the threat that was hovering over our heads, but I was anxious and kept secretly looking at my watch.

At four o'clock on the dot, there was a knock on the door.

My wife murmured, "Oh, no!"

At these two words, I realized that my machinations had not put her fears to rest either.

I opened the door with resignation. Our torturer was alone. He muttered a "Hello," handed me his coat, and, already accustomed to the routine, went to sit in his chair in the living room. He accepted a cup of coffee and said nothing.

I had the audacity to ask, as I had the day before, if his wife was going to come—not that I wanted to meet her particularly, but it would at least have provided a reason for his visit.

With a look of annoyance, he pulled out one of the big words from his repertory:

"No."

This was beginning to seem like a nightmare. At least our day's activity provided me with a brilliant topic of conversation:

"Did you notice? We put up a Christmas tree."

"Yes."

I almost asked, "It's pretty, isn't it?" but I attempted a scientific experiment with another bold question.

"How do you like it?"

No one could accuse me of indiscretion for this. I held my breath. The stakes were high: did Mr. Bernardin understand the notions of beauty and ugliness?

After his period of reflection and a vague glance at our work of art, we were treated to an ambiguous response, proffered with an empty voice:

"Okay."

"Okay": what did that mean in his internal lexicon? Did this word carry an aesthetic judgment, or was it ethical in nature? Did it mean that Christmas trees were in good taste? I persisted:

"What do you mean by 'okay'?"

The doctor looked irritated. I noticed that this expression came over him whenever my questions surpassed the lexical field of his usual responses. He nearly succeeded in making me feel ashamed, like the first two days, when I had actually believed that my questions were out of line. This time, I decided to resist:

"Does that mean you think it's pretty?"

"Yes."

Darn. I had forgotten not to give him a chance to slip in one of his two favorite words.

"What about you, do you have a Christmas tree?"

"No."

"Why?"

Our guest's face turned angry. That's it, look mad, I thought. It's true I'm asking you an unusually rude question: Why don't you have a tree? What a monster I am! And I won't help you out, this time. You'll have to find the answer on your own.

The seconds passed; Mr. Bernardin wrinkled his brow, either because he was thinking, or because he was ruminating his anger for having to confront an enigma worthy of the Sphinx. I was beginning to feel pretty good.

Imagine my surprise upon hearing Juliette suggest, in a kind voice, "Perhaps Mr. Bernardin doesn't know why he has no tree. One often doesn't know the reason for such things."

I looked at her disconsolately. She had foiled everything.

Out of the wood, our neighbor had recovered his serenity. Upon further inspection, I noticed that this word didn't suit him. There was nothing serene about him: I had associated this term with him because it was customarily used to describe fat people. But there was not a trace of such sweetness or coolness on the face of our torturer. Deep down, his face expressed nothing but sadness. It wasn't the kind of elegant sadness associated with the Portuguese; it was a heavy sadness, unflappable and endless, for you felt it was melted into his bulk.

Thinking about it, had I ever seen happy fat people? I searched my memory in vain. It struck me that the reputation for cheerfulness on the part of the obese was unfounded: on the contrary, most of them had the stricken appearance of Mr. Bernardin.

This had to be one of the reasons why his presence was unpleasant. If he had looked happy, I imagine his silence wouldn't have been so oppressive to me. There was something trying about the stagnation of this fleshy despair.

Juliette, who was even more fragile than she was petite, had a cheerful face even when she wasn't smiling. In the case of our guest, it must have been the opposite—assuming that he did smile on occasion.

Following the failure of the line of questioning on Christmas trees and their reasons for being or not being, I don't remember what I said anymore. I only know that it was long, very long and painful.

When he finally left, I couldn't believe it was six o'clock: I was positively certain it was nine o'clock, and I could foresee the moment when he was going to impose his presence for dinner. He had stayed "only" two hours, like the day before and the day before that.

With the injustice typical of those who are frustrated, I took it all out on my wife:

"Why did you come to his rescue about the Christmas tree? You should have let him flounder!"

"I came to his rescue?"

"Yes, you answered for him."

"That's because your question seemed a little out of place."

"It was! All the more reason to ask it. If only to test the level of his intelligence."

"He's a cardiologist, after all."

"Maybe he was intelligent in a past life. It's clear there's nothing's left of it now."

"Don't you have more the impression that he has a problem? He has an unhappy, fatalistic look about him."

"Listen, Juliette, you're a sweetheart, but we're not here to be good Samaritans."

"Do you think he's going to come back tomorrow?"

"How should I know?"

I realized that I was raising my voice, like the last of mediocrities.

"I'm sorry. That guy makes me crazy."

"If he comes back tomorrow, what will we do, Emile?"

"I don't know. What do you think?"

I felt despicable.

"Maybe he won't come back," she said with a smile.

"Maybe."

But I didn't believe it anymore.

. . .

The next day, at four o'clock in the afternoon, someone knocked on the door. We knew who it was.

Mr. Bernardin was silent. He seemed to find our lack of conversation the height of rudeness.

Two hours later, he went away.

. . .

"Tomorrow, Juliette, at ten till four, we'll go for a walk."

She chuckled.

The next day, at three-fifty, we set out on foot. It was snowing. We were delighted, we felt so free. Never had a walk given us so much joy.

My wife was ten years old. She threw her head back, face to the sky. She opened her mouth wide and tried to catch as many snowflakes as possible. She pretended to count them. From time to time, she announced a ridiculous number:

"Five hundred fifty-five."

"Liar."

In the forest, our steps made as little noise as the snow. We said nothing; we rediscovered that silence equals happiness.

Darkness soon fell. Thanks to the omnipresent whiteness, the brightness intensified. If silence were incarnated in matter, it would be snow.

It was after six when we returned to the House. The footsteps of a lone man, still recent, led to the door, then returned toward the neighbor's house. They made us laugh, in particular those that showed evidence of a long confounded wait on the doorstep. We had the impression we could read into these tracks, that we could picture Mr. Bernardin's look of discontentment. He must have thought that we were rude not to be there to welcome him.

Juliette was in a jovial mood. She seemed overexcited to me: the combination of this magical walk and the doctor's disappointment had put her in a state of mental intoxication. There had been so little in her life that she reacted to everything with intensity.

That night she slept badly. The next morning, she was coughing. I blamed myself: how could I have let her run bareheaded through the snow, swallowing hundreds of snowflakes?

It was nothing serious, but a walk that day would be out of the question.

I brought her an infusion in bed.

"Will he come today?"

We no longer had to specify who "he" was.

"Maybe he'll be discouraged by our absence yesterday."

"The other times we had put the light on in the living room at four o'clock. We could leave it off today."

"We didn't put it on yesterday, and it didn't stop him from coming."

"Deep down, when you think about it, Emile, do we have to open the door?"

I sighed, thinking that the truth always comes from the mouths of the innocent.

"You've asked the right question."

"You didn't answer."

"There's no law forcing us to open the door to him. It's a matter of politeness."

"Are we obliged to be polite?"

Again she was touching on a sensitive point.

"No one is obliged to be polite."

"So?"

"The problem, Juliette, is not our duty, but what's in our power."

"I don't understand."

"When you have sixty-five years of politeness behind you, are you capable of defying it?"

"Have we always been polite?"

"The simple fact that you are asking me that question proves to what extent our manners are rooted in us. We are so polite that our politeness has become unconscious. You can't fight your unconscious."

"Couldn't we try?"

"How?"

"If he knocks on the door and you're upstairs, it's under-standable that you wouldn't hear him. Especially at your age. It wouldn't even be rude."

"Why would I be upstairs?"

"Because I'm sick in bed, because you're staying by my bedside. Anyway, that's none of his business. There's nothing rude about being upstairs."

I knew she was right.

.   .   .

At four o'clock I was upstairs, sitting in the bedroom next to the patient. A knock sounded on the door.

"Juliette, I can hear him!"

"He doesn't know that. You could very well not hear him."

"At this hour?"

"Why not? I'm sick, you fell asleep keeping me company."

I was beginning to feel ill. My stomach was in a knot. My wife took my hand as if to give me courage.

"He'll stop soon."

That's where she was wrong. Not only didn't he stop, but he knocked louder and louder. I would have had to be on the fifth floor not to hear him. But the house had only two stories.

The minutes passed. Mr. Bernardin was at the point of drumming on our door like a madman.

"He's going to break it down."

"He's crazy. He should be locked up."

He was knocking louder and louder. I could picture his enormous mass beating against the surface, which would end up giving way. It would be unbearable not to have a door in this cold.

Then it reached a climax: he began banging on the door without stopping, at less than one-second intervals. I wouldn't have thought he had such strength. Juliette turned pale; she dropped my hand.

A terrible thing happened: at that moment, I raced down the stairs and opened the door.

The torturer's face was swelled with anger. I was so afraid I couldn't speak. I stood aside to allow him to enter. He took off his coat and went to sit in the chair he took to be his own.

"I didn't hear you," I ended up stammering.

"I knew you were here. The snow was fresh."

He had never spoken so many words in a row. Then he grew silent, exhausted. I was terrified. His statement proved that he wasn't an idiot; his attitude, however, was that of a dangerous madman.

An eternity later, he spoke another sentence:

"Yesterday, you weren't here."

The tone of his voice was accusatory.

"That's right. We went for a walk in the woods."

Here I was making excuses for myself! Ashamed at my cowardice, I forced myself to add, "You were knocking so loud. . . ."

You can't imagine the courage it took me to murmur these few words. But our neighbor felt no need for self-justification. He was knocking loud? Well, he was right, since it made me open the door!

The day had not yet come when I would have enough confidence to keep quiet.

"My wife caught a cold, yesterday, on our walk. She's in bed, she's coughing a little."

He was a doctor, after all. He might finally prove to be good for something. He was silent, however.

"Could you examine her?"

"She caught a cold," he responded with irritation, seeming to think, You're not going to bother me for that!

"It's nothing serious, but at our age . . ."

He no longer deigned to respond. The message was clear: for anything less than meningitis, we shouldn't expect his care.

He was silent again. I felt a surge of rage. What! I would have to devote two full hours to this idiot, who roused himself from his torpor only when it came to breaking down my door—and during this time, my poor sick wife would be alone in her bed! No, no, and no. I wouldn't tolerate it.

Courteously, I told him, "Would you please excuse me? Juliette needs me. You can sit in the living room or accompany me upstairs, as you wish. . . ."

Anybody would have understood that he was being asked to leave. Alas, Mr. Bernardin was not just anybody. Instead, I swear, he asked me, in a strangled voice, "You're not going to give me a cup of coffee?"

I couldn't believe my ears. So the cup of coffee that we had offered him every day out of courtesy had become his due! With a certain terror, I realized that everything we had granted him, from the first visit, had become his due: in his primitive brain, a kindness offered once attained the status of law.

I wasn't going to serve it to him, was I? That would have taken the cake. It seems Americans say to their guests, "Help yourself." But you can't just become an American at will. At the same time, I didn't have the nerve to refuse him anything. With my characteristic lack of audacity, I offered him a middle ground:

"I don't have time to make coffee, but since I have to boil water for my wife's infusion, I can serve you a cup of tea."

I almost added, "If that's okay with you," but I had the basic courage to edit myself.

After serving him his tea, I brought an infusion up to Juliette. Curled in her bed, she whispered to me, "What's wrong with him? Why was he knocking on the door like a savage?"

Her eyes were wide with fear.

"I don't know. But don't worry, he's not dangerous."

"Are you sure? You heard how hard he was banging on the poor door."

"He's not violent, he's just uncouth."

I told her that he had demanded his coffee. She burst out laughing.

"Why don't you just leave him alone downstairs?"

"I don't dare."

"Try. Just to see his reaction."

"I don't want him to start going through our things."

"That's not his style."

"What is his style?"

"Listen, he's a boor. You have the right to be a boor with a boor. Anyway, don't go downstairs, please. I'm afraid for you to be alone with him."

I smiled.

"Are you less afraid when you're there to protect me?"

At that instant, we heard a terrible crash. Then another similar one, then a third. The rhythm confirmed what was happening: the enemy was climbing the stairs. The steps were accustomed to our light bodies; Mr. Bernardin's mass was making them scream.

Juliette and I looked at each other like children locked in a monster's pantry. No escape was possible. The slow, heavy steps grew nearer. I had left the door open and didn't even think of closing it now: what would be the point of this meager defense? We were lost.

At that very moment, I was aware of the absurdity of our fear: we weren't actually at any great risk. Our neighbor was a pest, for sure, but he wouldn't hurt us. Yet somehow that didn't stop us from feeling terrified. We could already feel his presence. To play the game, I took the hand of the patient and assumed a meditative pose.

Here he was. He was gazing at the scene: the concerned husband, seated at the bedside of his suffering wife. I acted surprised.

"Oh! You came up?"

As if the noise of the staircase could have left any doubt!

The expression on his face resisted analysis. It seemed both outraged at our ill manners and suspicious: Juliette could be pretending to be sick with the goal of falling short on her duty to be courteous toward him.

With comic gratitude, she groaned:

"Oh, doctor, how kind of you! But I think I've simply caught cold."

Taken aback, he came to pose his hand on her forehead. I looked at him in astonishment: his brain had to be functioning if he was examining my wife! What would come out of it?

He finally removed his fat hand. He didn't speak. In the space of an instant, I imagined the worst.

"Well, doctor?"

"Nothing. There's nothing wrong with her."

"But she's coughing!"

"Probably a little inflammation of the throat. But there's nothing wrong with her."

This sentence, which a normal doctor would have spoken in a reassuring voice, sounded in his mouth as if he were registering an insult—"For this faker you're refusing to tend to me?"

I pretended not to notice anything.

"Thank you, doctor, thank you! I'm so relieved. How much do I owe you?"

To pay him for placing his hand on my wife's forehead might seem strange: mainly, I just didn't want to be beholden to him.

He shrugged his shoulders in a churlish fashion. And thus I discovered a character trait of our torturer—and the simple fact that he had a character trait surprised me: money didn't interest him. Was it possible there was room in him for flashes, if not of nobility, at least of an absence of vulgarity?

True to form, he hastened to leave no trace of this start of a favorable impression. He crossed the room and settled into a chair, facing us.

Juliette and I exchanged a look of incredulity: was he going to besiege us even in our bedroom? The situation was as hellish as it was without exit. We were cornered.

Even supposing that I were capable of kicking someone out, how would I have proceeded with him? Especially since he had just examined my wife for free!

The latter finally ventured, "Doctor, you . . . you're not going to stay here?"

A note of shock passed over his mournful face. What! What was she daring to say to him?

"This is no place to entertain you. You'll be bored."

He seemed to accept this. But he uttered these crushing words:

"If I go to the living room, you have to come too."

Distraught, I made a vain effort:

"I can't leave her alone."

"She's not sick."

This surpassed the wildest imagination! I simply repeated, "I can't leave her alone!"

"She's not sick."

"But doctor, she's delicate! At our age, it's only normal!"

"She's not sick."

I looked at Juliette. She shook her head in resignation. If

only I had had the strength to declare, "Sick or not sick, I'm staying with her! Get out of here!" I realized the extent to which I belonged to the race of the weak. I hated myself.

I stood up, defeated, and went down to the living room with Mr. Bernardin, leaving my poor coughing wife in the bedroom.

The intruder collapsed into his armchair. He took the cup of tea I had made him before going upstairs. He brought it to his lips, then handed it to me, saying, "Now it's cold."

I'm not making up a word of this. I was taken aback for a moment, then an insane feeling of mirth came over me: this was outrageous! To be this rude was unthinkable. I laughed and laughed, and half an hour of tension melted in this hilarity.

I took the cup from the hands of this fat man, who was angered by my glee, and headed for the kitchen.

"I'll make you a new cup right away."

·   ·   ·

At six o'clock, he left. I went upstairs.

"I heard you laughing loudly."

I told her about the cold tea. She laughed too. Afterward, she seemed distressed.

"Emile, what are we going to do?"

"I don't know."

"We mustn't open the door to him anymore."

"You saw what happened earlier. He'll break the door down if I don't open it for him."

"So let him break the door down! That'll gives us a wonderful reason to have a falling-out with him."

"But the door will be broken. In winter!"

"We'll repair it."

"But it'll get broken for nothing, because there's no way to have a falling-out with him. Besides, it would be better to remain on good terms: he's our neighbor."

"So?"

"It's best to get along with one's neighbors."

"Why?"

"It's customary. And don't forget that we're alone here. What's more, he's a doctor."

"We wanted to be alone. You say he's a doctor, but I think he's going to make us sick."

"Let's not exaggerate. He's harmless."

"Don't you see how anxious we are after a few days? What state will we be in, in a month, in six months?"

"Maybe he'll stop at the end of winter."

"You know he won't. He'll come every day, every day, from four o'clock to six o'clock."

"Maybe he'll get discouraged."

"He'll never get discouraged."

I sighed.

"Listen, it's true he's annoying. But we have a nice life here, don't we? It's the life we've always wanted. We're not going to let it be poisoned by such a ridiculous detail. There are twenty-four hours in a day. Two hours is a twelfth of a day. Basically nothing. We have twenty-two hours of happiness daily. How can we complain? Have you considered the fate of those who don't even have two hours of happiness a day?"

"Is that any reason to allow ourselves to be invaded?"

"Decency forces us to compare our lives to those of others. Our existence is a dream. I would be ashamed to complain."

"It's not fair. You worked forty years for a small salary. Our happiness today is modest and deserved. We've already paid the price."

"You can't reason like that. Nothing is ever deserved."

"How does that prevent us from defending ourselves?"

"To defend ourselves against a poor idiot, a flabby brute of a man? Better to laugh about it, don't you think?"

"I can't laugh about it."

"You're wrong. It's easy to laugh about it. From now on, we'll laugh about Mr. Bernardin."

. . .

The next day, Juliette was better. At four in the afternoon, there was a knock on the door. I went to open it, a smile on my lips. We had decided to welcome him with all the mockery he deserved.

"Oh! What a surprise!" I exclaimed upon discovering our torturer.

He stepped inside grumpily and handed me his coat. Ecstatic, I continued:

"Juliette, you'll never guess who's here!"

"Who is it?" she asked, from the top of the stairs.

"It's the wonderful Palamedes Bernardin! Our charming neighbor!"

My wife descended the steps cheerfully.

"The doctor? Well, I'll be!"

In her voice, I could hear her restraining a laugh. She took his plump hand in hers and pressed it to her heart.

"Oh, thank you doctor! Feel, I'm all cured. And I owe it to you."

The fat man seemed uneasy. He took his hand from my wife's and walked resolutely to his armchair, collapsing into it.

"Would you like a cup of coffee?"

"Yes."

"What else can I offer you? Do you realize you saved my life yesterday? What would you like?"

Immobile, he said nothing.

"An almond cookie? Apple pie?"

We didn't have any of that at home. I was wondering if Juliette wasn't going overboard. At least she seemed to be having fun. She continued her enumeration of imaginary sweets:

"A big slice of fruitcake? A piece of meringue? Scottish pudding? An upside-down strawberry cheesecake? Chocolate éclairs?"

I doubted whether she had ever seen such desserts in her life. The doctor was beginning to get his angry look. After a long, hostile silence, he said, "Coffee!"

Ignoring his rudeness, my wife exclaimed, "Nothing? Really? That's too bad. It would bring me such pleasure to pamper you. Thanks to you, doctor, I've been reborn!"

Light as a kid, she ran to the kitchen. What would she have done had our guest accepted one of the cakes? In a bantering mood, I went to sit down next to him.

"My dear Palamedes, what do you think of Chinese taxonomy?"

He said nothing. He didn't even act surprised. His tired expression could be interpreted as follows: "Am I going to be subjected to the tiresome conversation of this one again?"

I resolved to be oppressive:

"Borges is staggering on this subject. Allow me to quote this well-known passage from his *Other Inquisitions*: 'In the distant pages of a certain Chinese encyclopedia entitled *The*

44

Celestial Market of Benevolent Knowledge, it is written that animals are divided into a) belonging to the Emperor, b) embalmed, c) tamed, d) milk pigs, e) mermaids, f) the fabulous, g) wild dogs, h) included in the present classification, i) agitated like madmen, j) innumerable, k) drawn with a very fine camel hair brush, l) et cetera, m) that have just broken the jug, n) which from afar seem like flies.' Doesn't this classification prompt a smile, if not out-and-out laughter, from a scientist of your caliber?"

I guffawed in the most civilized fashion. Mr. Bernardin remained like a stone.

"That said, I know people who aren't the slightest bit amused by it. And it's true that, beyond the comic side of the matter, this example illustrates the thorny problem of taxonomic procedure. There's no reason to imagine that our mental categories are any less absurd that those of the Chinese."

Juliette served us coffee.

"Perhaps you're fatiguing our dear doctor with your terribly obscure reflections. . . ."

"You can't have read Aristotle without reflecting on these questions, Juliette. And it's impossible to read this delicious exercise in incongruity without remembering it."

"Perhaps you should explain to the doctor who Aristotle is."

"Excuse her, Palamedes, she had no doubt forgotten the

45

role played by Aristotle in the history of medicine. Deep down, the very idea of the category is incredible. Where did man's need to classify reality come from? I'm not talking about dualisms, which are quasi-natural transpositions of the original dichotomy, namely the male-female opposition. In fact, the term *category* can only be justified from the moment when there are more than two points—a binary classification doesn't merit this name. Do you know who is credited with the first ternary classification—and thus the first categorization in history—and from when it dates?"

The torturer was drinking his coffee. He seemed to be thinking, Keep yapping.

"You'll never guess: Tachandrus of Lydia. Do you realize what that means? Nearly two centuries before Aristotle! What humiliation for the Stagirite! Have you even thought about what occurred in Tachandrus's head? For the first time, a human being had the idea of distributing reality as a function of an abstract order—that's right, abstract. We don't think about it today, but at its core, any division by a number greater than two is abstraction pure and simple. If there had been three sexes, the abstraction would have begun at division by four, and so on."

Juliette was watching me in admiration.

"That's extraordinary! You've never been so fascinating!"

"I was waiting, my dearest, to have a man of my caliber with whom to converse!"

"What luck that you came, doctor! Without you, I would never have known anything about this Tachandrus of Lydia."

"Let's go back to this first experiment in taxonomy. Do you know what Tachandrus's categorization consisted of? It resulted from his observations of the animal world. Indeed, our Lydian was a kind of zoologist. He divided animals into three species, which he called animals with feathers, animals with fur, and—get this—animals with skin. The latter class included the batrachians, reptiles, men, and fish—I'm citing them in the order of his treatise. Isn't that marvelous? I love that antique wisdom by which the human is an animal among others."

"I agree with him. Man is an animal!" added my wife enthusiastically.

"Right away, several questions are raised. Where does Tachandrus put insects and crustaceans? It turns out that for him, they're not animals! To his eyes, insects belong to the world of dust—with the exception of the dragonfly and the butterfly, which he classifies among the animals with feathers. As for crustaceans, he sees them as articulated shells. And shells are minerals, according to him. What poetry!"

"And flowers? Where does he put them?"

"Let's not mix things up, Juliette; we're talking about animals. One might also wonder how the Lydian managed not to notice that man was hairy. And conversely, that furry

47

animals had what we call a skin. It's very strange. His criteria are rather impressionistic. Because of that, biologists naturally ridiculed Tachandrus. No one bothers to notice that he represents an unprecedented intellectual and metaphysical leap. Because his ternary system is in no way a dyad disguised as a triad."

"What is that, Emile, a dyad disguised as a triad?"

"Well, for example, if he had divided animals into heavy, light, and medium. Hegel didn't do any better. . . . What went on, then, in the mind of the Lydian, at the moment when he thought of this? The question is very exciting to me. Did his first intuition include a vision of three criteria, or did he begin with an ordinary dichotomy—feathers and fur—and realize in the process that it wasn't enough? This we'll never know."

Mr. Bernardin's expression was that of a shoemaker lost in Byzantium: sovereign disdain. But he remained immobile in "his" armchair.

"Biologists are wrong to laugh at him. Has zoology today developed more intelligent classifications? You see, Palamedes, when Juliette and I decided to live in the country, I bought a book on ornithology—a matter of familiarizing myself with my new environment."

I rose to get the book.

"Here it is: *Birds of the World*, Bordas Publishers, 1994. It describes birds, beginning with the ninety-nine families of nonsparrows and ending with the seventy-four families of sparrows. This system is preposterous. There's something staggering about describing a being starting with what it isn't. What would happen if we decided to first try to mention everything that a being isn't?"

"That's true!" said my wife.

"Imagine, my dear friend, that I got it into my head to describe you by first enumerating everything that you're not! It would be insane. 'Everything that Palamedes Bernardin isn't.' The list would be long, because there are plenty of things that you're not. Where would I begin?"

"For instance, one could say that the doctor isn't an animal with feathers!"

"Indeed. And he's neither a pest, nor a boor, nor an idiot."

Juliette's eyes grew wide. She turned pale and put her hand over her mouth as if to stifle her laughter.

The face of our guest, meanwhile, showed nothing. I had attentively observed his features as I uttered this last statement. Nothing. Not the slightest flash in his eyes. He didn't even blink. Yet there was no doubt he had heard me. I must confess I was impressed.

As a result, I was the one who had to land on my feet. I continued at random:

"It's strange that the problem of taxonomy appeared by

way of biology. It's true that it might be a logical inevitability: no one would go to the trouble of inventing categories for things with as little variety as thunder. It's the multiple and the disparate that create the need for classification. And what could be more disparate and multiple than animals and vegetables? But we can find even deeper affinities in them. . . ."

Suddenly I realized that these affinities, to which I had given so much thought, had escaped me. I was incapable of remembering the result of twenty years of reflection, despite the fact that no later than the day before I still remembered them. It must have been the presence, or rather the oppression, of Mr. Bernardin that was blocking my brain.

"What are the affinities?" inquired my wife.

"I'm still at the stage of hypotheses, but I'm sure they exist. What do you think, Palamedes?"

Wait as we might, he wouldn't respond. I couldn't help but admire him; whether or not he was an idiot, he had the courage, or the nerve, that I had never had: to answer nothing. Neither "I don't know," nor a shrug of the shoulders. Absolute indifference. On the part of a man who imposed his presence at my home for hours, it was on the order of the miraculous. I was fascinated. I envied his ability. He didn't even seem bothered—only we were! It was unbelievable!

I was wrong to be surprised, in fact: if boors were

ashamed of their manners, they wouldn't be boors. I caught myself thinking how great it must be to be a brute. What a triumph: to allow oneself every indelicacy and let others feel regret, as if they were the ones who had behaved badly!

The prodigious ease with which I had begun the conversation quickly faded. I kept up the act, continuing a ceaseless monologue on God knows which pre-Socratic, but I could feel I was no longer in a position of strength.

Was it my imagination? I seemed to perceive an expression pass over the face of our neighbor that could be translated in these terms: "Why are you going to so much trouble? I won, you can't help but see that. Isn't the simple fact that I besiege your living room every day for two hours the proof? Brilliant as your discourse may be, you can't deny the evidence: I'm in your home, and I'm bothering you."

At six o'clock, he left.

·   ·   ·

I couldn't sleep. Juliette noticed that I was awake. She must have suspected what I was thinking, because she said, "You were terrific this afternoon."

"At the time, that's what I thought. But I'm not so sure anymore."

"All your philosophical considerations coming down to letting him know that he's a pest! I almost applauded."

51

"Perhaps. But what good did it do?"

"You impressed him."

"You can't impress a man like that."

"You saw that he was incapable of responding to you."

"But we were the ones who were bothered by it, not him. Nothing bothers him."

"How can you know what goes on in his heart of hearts?"

"Even imagining that something does go on, that doesn't change our problem: in the end, he's still sitting in our living room."

"I had fun, anyway."

"I'm glad at least for that."

"Should we do it again tomorrow?"

"Yes. Because there's no alternative. I doubt your exaggerated courtesy and my riot of erudition will manage to unseat him, but at least they'll distract us."

That's what we had come to.

. . .

The advantage of nuisances is they push you 'til your back is to the wall. I, who had never been introspective, surprised myself exploring my innermost depths, hoping to find as-yet-untapped strength.

For want of finding any, I learned many things about myself. For example, I hadn't realized that I was a coward. In forty years of teaching at the high school, I had never had to deal with the slightest commotion. The students respected me. I suppose that I benefited from a certain authority natural to teachers. But I had been wrong to deduce that I was one of the strong. In truth, I was one of the civilized: in their company, I was entirely at ease. It had sufficed for me to find myself confronted with a brutish lout to see the limits of my power.

I was searching for memories that could be useful to me; I came across many that weren't. The mind has incomprehensible systems of defense: you call on it for help, and instead of assisting you, it sends up pretty images. And in the end it's not wrong, for while these pretty images don't solve your problems, they serve as salvation for the moment. Memory behaves like the tie merchant in the desert: "Water? No, but I've got a large selection of ties if you'd like." In this case, it was: "How to get rid of an oppressor? No idea, but do you remember those autumn roses you liked so much several years ago? . . ."

Juliette was ten years old. We were city children. My wife, at ten, had the longest hair in the school. Its color and luster were on the order of fine leather. We had already been married four years. This wedding had been recognized by the entire universe, beginning with our parents—especially by mine, who were broad-minded.

They sometimes invited my wife to sleep at our house—the reverse never occurred, for her parents considered that it was "too soon." I found this restriction perplexing, since they knew that their daughter often spent the night at my house. The transgression was therefore accepted in my house and not in hers. I thought this was strange but said nothing, so as not to hurt Juliette.

My parents weren't rich: we had a shower, but no bathtub. For this reason, a bath is still synonymous with luxury to me. The shower room wasn't heated, and I've retained this memory, though why I like it so much puzzles me. Juliette and I had washed together since our marriage, without it having aroused me in the slightest: my wife's nudity was part of the natural phenomena, along with the rain and the sunset, and it would never have occurred to me to see it as erotic.

Except in winter. At night, we showered together before going to bed. We had to undress in this freezing room, which was quite an adventure. Each time we took off a piece of clothing, we screamed from the cold, which pierced through us more and more. By the time we were naked, we were nothing but a long cry of glacial suffering.

We slipped behind the shower curtain, and I turned on the faucet. The water ran, arctic cold at first, which gave rise to a new volley of shouting. My prepubescent wife rolled herself in the plastic curtain for protection. An instant later, the shower began spitting a burning rain, and we voiced our shock in shrill laughter.

I was the man. I was therefore the one who had to adjust the water's temperature. It was a complicated task; the slightest brush against the faucet caused the stream to go from boiling to freezing or vice versa. It took at least ten minutes of trial and error to obtain a tolerable heat. In the meantime, Juliette, draped in her plastic cloak, laughed in horror at each change of direction.

When the water was just right, I extended my hand for her to join me under the stream. The curtain unraveled to reveal the white slenderness of a ten-year-old, topped by an enormous head of chestnut hair. Her grace took my breath away.

She came to huddle under the liquid beam and moaned with pleasure because I had regulated the temperature to perfection. I took her long hair and wet it, flabbergasted to see its volume shrink beneath the water. I squeezed it as if to make a rope. Her straight back then appeared in all its paleness, with protruding shoulder blades that resembled folded wings.

I took a piece of soap and rubbed it on her hair until it lathered. I gathered it in a mass on top of her head, kneaded and molded it into a crown larger than her skull. Then I soaped her body; when I passed between her thighs, Juliette let out piercing cries because I was tickling her.

Then we rinsed ourselves for hours. We felt too good

under this warm stream of water; we had no desire to leave. It had to be done, however: I shut off the faucet all at once, my wife pulled back the curtain, and a burst of cold air hit us. We screamed in unison and grabbed the towels.

I had to rub Juliette to stop her from turning blue. She laughed, her teeth chattering, saying, "I'm going to die." She slipped on her long, white nightshirt and begged me to join her in bed quickly to warm her up.

I would arrive in the bedroom and see only the wet hair sticking out of the quilt. It was the only tangible sign of her presence: her slim body wasn't large enough to cause a hump in the down. I climbed in next to her and saw her joking face. "I'm cold," she'd say. I would take her in my arms, squeeze her tight, and blow hot air on her neck.

Thus, my only childhood memories that one could call erotic are linked with winter. What strikes me is their continual alternation of pain and pleasure: as if I needed the suffering of the cold in order to discover not only the adorable charms of my ten-year-old wife, but also the means to enjoy them.

I realize now that they are the best memories of my childhood and thus of my life.

Why the devil did I need a torturer to find such a treasure in my mind?

.   .   .

Juliette's hair was white, and she had cut it short. Except for that, she hadn't changed. Nothing about her suggested aging. Instead, she appeared as if she had emerged from a long illness in which she had left her tresses behind.

What remained of her hair now was a ravishing color that seemed artificial: it had the bluish whiteness of a romantic tutu.

And soft! A softness that was not of this world. Even the down of a baby would be scratchy by comparison. This must be what angel hair is like.

Angels don't have children, and neither does Juliette. She is her own child—and mine.

. . .

You can't imagine how slowly days pass. The entire world claims that time passes quickly, but it's false.

It was more false than ever during this month of January. To be more specific, every period of the day had its rhythm: the evenings were long and sweet, the mornings short and full of hope. In the early afternoon, an unspoken anxiety accelerated the cadence of minutes to a staggering degree. And at four o'clock, time nearly stopped.

Unfortunately, the stretch devoted to Mr. Bernardin ended up becoming the bulk of our days. We didn't dare admit it to one another, but we knew we were in agreement on this point.

I had opted for gallantry. Since our guest imposed on us and said nothing, wasn't it logical that I should shower him in a flood of uninterrupted and tedious words? Uninterrupted so that I wouldn't bore myself, and tedious so that I would bore him.

I must admit that I occasionally took pleasure in this exercise. I who had never spoken much in society, was now forced to do so—assuming that one could qualify the doctor as society. My experience as a teacher was a help, but there was an essential difference: at the high school, I would strive to get my students' attention. In my living room, it was the opposite: I tried to be as dull as possible.

In this way I discovered an unsuspected truth: it is far more entertaining to be boring than to be interesting. In class, when I tried to present a lively image of Cicero, I would sometimes have to stifle an inner yawn. Yet when I barraged our torturer with my stodgy erudition, I could barely contain my jubilation. I finally understood why lecturers are nearly always boring.

Since I was just starting out in my profession as a bore, it happened on occasion that I drew blanks. I filled in as best I could. One day, after pontificating on Hesiod for an hour, I found myself facing a void. The devil took advantage to inspire this nosy question in me:

"And Mrs. Bernardin?"

The neighbor took some time to react, and for once I could sympathize with him: to be questioned about one's wife when five seconds earlier the topic was Hesiod would be enough to throw anyone off.

He didn't respond, in fact. He merely looked at me with an outraged expression. I didn't let it get to me, however, because I had become aware of a general truth: there was never a time when Palamedes Bernardin didn't look un-happy.

I pushed the matter:

"Yes. It gives us great pleasure to see you every day, as you know. But we would be even happier if your wife would agree to accompany you."

I was thinking, in fact, that the presence of his other half couldn't worsen the situation. And since our guest didn't seem to appreciate my suggestion, I found it all the better.

"I know your proverbial delicacy, Palamedes. What would you say to bringing her for tea or coffee tomorrow after-noon?"

Silence.

"Juliette would be delighted to have female company. What is Mrs. Bernardin's first name?"

Fifteen seconds of reflection.

"Bernadette."

"Bernadette Bernardin?"

59

I burst out in an idiotic giggle, delighted at my rudeness.

"Palamedes and Bernadette Bernardin. An odd first name united with an ordinary but repetitive first name. Marvelous."

An unexpected thing happened: our neighbor took a position.

"She won't come."

"Oh, pardon me, I offended you. Please excuse me. Your first names are charming."

"That's not it."

He had rarely spoken so much.

"Is she sick?"

"No."

Aware of and pleased with my indiscretion, I continued:

"Do you get along well with her?"

"Yes."

"In that case, don't argue, Palamedes! Come, it's decided. And to force you to introduce us to your wife, we'll invite you to join us not for tea but for dinner, tomorrow, at eight o'clock. As I'm sure you know, to refuse a dinner invitation is very impolite."

Juliette came out of the kitchen to gaze at me in horror. I reassured her with a glance and continued without hesitation.

"The only thing is, since we will need to devote ourselves to the preparations for such a special occasion, we shall have to ask you, dear Palamedes, not to visit with us tomorrow afternoon. Just this once, we'll wait until evening to see one another."

Juliette went back inside the kitchen to hide her amusement.

Mr. Bernardin was baffled. It was no doubt for this reason that a miracle happened: he left at five minutes to six. I was thrilled.

My wife and I, under the shock of his mortification as much as of our absurd invitation, were doubled over with laughter for quite a while.

"We should invite them every evening, in fact, Emile. We'd have our afternoons free."

"That's an idea. But let's wait to discover the charms of Bernadette Bernardin. I imagine her to be most divine."

"She couldn't be worse than her husband."

We were sincerely impatient to see.

. . .

Juliette awoke at five in the morning. She was so excited by the circumstance that it worried me.

With her six-year-old's smile, she asked me, "What if we were to make some disgusting food?"

"No. Don't forget that we'll have to eat it as well."

"You think so?"

"How can we avoid it? In any case, that wouldn't be a

good strategy. Better to make them uncomfortable with exaggerated splendor. We should wear exceedingly elegant clothes and serve oppressively fine food."

"But . . . we have neither the clothes nor the ingredients for such splendor."

"In a manner of speaking. The goal is that we'll be too good for them. And we are."

We were. The living room was cleaned and polished to excess. We spent the afternoon cooking. Come evening, we dressed in garments that were as inappropriate as possible.

Juliette chose a velvet sheath dress that accentuated her slenderness.

It is said that promptness is the chivalry of kings. But what kind of king would have promptness for his sole courtesy? The answer would be our neighbor, who always arrived on time to the minute.

At eight o'clock on the dot, there was a knock on the door.

.   .   .

Mr. Bernardin gave the impression of being slim and talkative. Had he lost weight? Had he learned to speak? Not at all.

But we had met his wife.

A long time ago, we had gone to see Fellini's *Satyricon.*

Juliette had not let go of my hand, as if *The Return of the Living Dead* were being projected. At the moment when the hermaphrodite is discovered in the grotto, I thought she was going to leave the theater, she was so afraid.

When Mrs. Bernardin entered the room, we stopped breathing. She was as terrifying as the Fellinian creature. Not that she looked like it, far from it, but she too was at the limit of human.

The neighbor crossed our threshold, then extended his hand outside, drawing inside something enormous and slow. It was a mass of flesh wearing a dress, or rather, that had been wrapped in a piece of fabric.

We had to face facts: as there was no one else with the doctor, it had to be concluded that this protuberance was called Bernadette Bernardin.

When it comes down to it, the word *protuberance* wasn't right. Its fat was too smooth and white to evoke that kind of eruption.

A cyst, this thing was a cyst. Eve grew out of Adam's rib. Mrs. Bernardin had no doubt grown like a cyst in the belly of our torturer. Sometimes an internal cyst is removed from a patient that amounts to twice, or three times, his weight: Palamedes had married just such an accumulation of flesh.

This explanation was pure lucubration on my part, it's true. Yet, all in all, it seemed more reasonable than the rational version: that this swelling could have, one day, been a woman—enough of a woman so that her hand had been asked in marriage. No. The mind could not accept such a possibility.

This was not the moment to think: we had to welcome the husband and wife into our home. Juliette behaved like a pro. She approached the cyst and extended her hand, saying, "Dear madame, what a pleasure to meet you."

To my surprise, a fleshy tentacle detached itself from the mass and allowed itself to be touched by my wife's fingers. I didn't have the courage to imitate her. I led the two heavy-weights into the living room.

Madame was hunched on the couch. Monsieur sat in his chair. They stopped moving and grew silent.

We were aghast. Especially me, since I was responsible for this invasion—for this intrusion of flesh under our roof. And to think that I had taken this initiative in order to make our neighbor uncomfortable!

Bernadette didn't have a nose; vague holes served in place of nostrils. Narrow slits situated above contained ocular globes: perhaps they were eyes, though there was no indication they could see. What intrigued me the most was her mouth: it looked like that of an octopus. I wondered whether this orifice had the faculty to produce sounds.

Very civilly, I addressed her with a naturalness that surprised even me.

"My dear madame, what can I serve you? A kir? A touch of sherry? Some port?"

A terrifying thing happened: the mass turned toward her husband and belched some muffled grunts. Palamedes, who seemed to understand these rumblings, translated:

"No alcohol."

Disconcerted, I persisted:

"A fruit juice? Orange, apple, tomato?"

A new round of noises. The interpreter transmitted:

"A glass of milk. Warm and without sugar."

After ten seconds of uneasiness, he added, "A kir for me."

Juliette and I were all too happy to have a reason to take refuge in the kitchen. We didn't dare look at one another as she heated the milk. To break the tension, I murmured, "Should we serve it to her in a bottle?"

Convulsive laughter from the little girl with white hair.

The tentacle of flesh brushed against my hand when I handed it the glass. A shudder of disgust ran through me.

This was nothing compared with the repulsion that clenched my jaws when the glass was inserted into the mouth. The orifice folded back what served as lips and began to inhale. The milk was sucked in all at once, but ingested in several gulps; each swallow made the noise of a rubber plunger unclogging a drain.

I was horrified. Quick, speak, say something.

"How long have you been married?"

When I let my unconscious express itself, it was always indiscreet.

After fifteen seconds, the husband responded:

"Forty-five years."

Forty-five years with this cyst. I was beginning to understand the mental state of this man a little better.

"Two years longer than we have," I said with admiration for their conjugal longevity.

I felt that my voice rang false. As a result, I could no longer control my words, causing me to ask this monstrous question:

"Do you have children?"

A second later, I cursed myself. Does one have children with . . . that? Nonetheless, I was flabbergasted by Mr. Bernardin's reaction. He turned red with anger and said in a furious voice, "You already asked me that question! The first day!"

He was panting with rage. Apparently what made him furious was not the thoughtless cruelty of my question, but the fact that he had already answered it. In the light of this explosion, I realized how exceptional our torturer's memory was—a faculty that served no purpose other than to make him angry when he caught someone else's memory faltering.

I muttered an excuse. Silence. I no longer dared speak. I couldn't stop myself from contemplating Mrs. Bernardin. I had always been taught not to stare at abnormal people, but it was stronger than I was.

I noticed that this thing, which must have been seventy years old, didn't show her age. Her skin—well, the membrane that encased her—was smooth and wrinkle-free. Her head was covered with beautiful black hair, healthy and without a hint of gray.

The voice of an internal demon whispered to me, "Yes, Bernadette is fresh as a baby." I bit my lip to hold back an urge to chuckle. It was then that I noticed the sky blue ribbon with which someone—Palamedes no doubt—had tied up several locks of her hair. This coquetry got the better of me: I began hiccuping in a pathetic, sickly manner.

When I had the strength to stop, I saw that Mr. Bernardin was staring at me discontentedly.

The adorable Juliette flew to my rescue:

"Emile, can you tend to the dinner? Thank you, you're an angel."

When I was safe inside the kitchen, I heard her launch into a long monologue:

"Have you noticed how kind my husband is? He treats me like a princess. And it's been this way since I was six years old. It's true, we were both six years old when we met. We loved one another from the first second, and we've never been apart. In fifty-nine years of life together, we have

67

never ceased to be happy with one another. Emile is an exceptionally intelligent and cultured man. He could have gotten bored with me, but not at all! We have only good memories. When I was young, I had very long chestnut hair. He was the one who took care of it: he washed it and styled it. No teacher of Greek and Latin has ever been such a good hairdresser. The day of our marriage, he made me a gorgeous bun. Here, look at the photograph. We were twenty-three years old. Emile was so handsome! He still is, in fact. Do you know that I kept my wedding dress? Sometimes I still wear it. I thought of wearing it this evening, but you might have found that strange. I didn't have any children either, madame, and I don't regret it. The world today is so hard for young people. In our day, it was easy. We were born one month apart: he on December 5, 1929; I on January 5, 1930. We were fifteen years old at the end of the war. It's so lucky that we weren't any older! Emile would have had to go off into combat and might have died. I could never have lived without him. You understand that, don't you? You've lived such a long time together too."

I stuck my head out to witness the spectacle. Juliette was talking animatedly by herself while the torturer was looking into the void. As for the one sitting next to him, it was impossible to know what she was doing.

We had to move to the table. Seating Mrs. Bernardin was

an ordeal. Two-thirds of her mass spilled over the chair. Would she fall on her side, we wondered? To avoid such a collapse, we wedged the seat as close as possible to the table. That way, her chair was stuck. But it was best not to focus on the ring of fat that spread around her plate.

This happened a year ago, and I don't remember what we served. I remember only that we had carefully prepared the most refined menu possible. Casting pearls before swine? Worse. Piglets eat anything without discretion, but they seem to derive a kind of pleasure from it.

The neighbor, however, ate avidly and with disgust. He gobbled down large quantities while seeming to find the food revolting. He didn't comment on a single dish. During the meal, he uttered only one sentence—of surprising length for him:

"You eat so much and stay thin!"

He thrust this at us angrily. I almost replied that it was hardly possible for us to eat very much, given the little food they had left us. I was wise enough to keep this remark to myself.

Mrs. Bernardin's movements were extremely slow. I considered helping her cut the meat, but she managed on her own. It was her mouth, in fact, that performed the work of a knife. She brought enormous chunks to the orifice, and a kind of beaklike lip cut off a portion. The tentacle then redescended in slow motion to the plate and deposited the surplus, which ended up looking like a food sculpture.

There was something graceful about this dance. It was the subsequent activities of her mouth that made you want to vomit. I won't describe them.

At least you could give her the benefit of the doubt: it was possible that she took pleasure in eating. The face of her husband, on the other hand, revealed only anger: how could anyone cook this badly? Which didn't stop him from finishing off the platter, with a look that said, "Someone has to do it."

Juliette must have thought the same thing, because she asked the following question:

"What do you eat normally, sir?"

Fifteen seconds of reflection led to this sentence:

"Soup."

That could mean anything, but it was all we were going to learn. Ask as we might, "What kind of soup? Clear, clarified, fish, pea, vegetable, cream, cold, squash, leek, with croutons, with meat, with noodles, with grated cheese . . . ?" the only answer we received, at intervals, was, "Soup."

I assumed, nonetheless, that he was the one who cooked it. No doubt we were asking too much of him.

Dessert was a catastrophe. It was therefore, and not surprisingly, the only dish I remember: cream puffs with a saucer of melted chocolate. The cyst got excited at the sight and smell of the chocolate. She wanted to keep the saucer and leave us the pastries. Juliette and I were open to the idea, wishing mostly to avoid a scandal. It was Mr. Bernardin who intervened.

We witnessed a conjugal spat of the third kind. The doctor rose and authoritatively deposited several cream puffs onto his spouse's plate. Then he coated them with a reasonable portion of chocolate and put the saucer out of reach. As soon as the object of her desire was taken away, the wife produced a wailing sound that had nothing human about it. The tentacles stretched as far as they could toward the Grail. The doctor took the saucer and hugged it, saying in a firm voice, "No. You can't. No."

Howling from Bernadette.

My wife murmured, "You can give it to her, sir. I can melt some more chocolate, it's easy."

This suggestion was ignored. The volume grew louder between the Bernardins. He shouted, "No!" and she shouted something that seemed to be in a dialect. Little by little, we identified the sound:

"Soup! Soup!"

It seemed she thought she was dealing with a variation on her staple. I was stupid enough to say, "No, madame, it's not soup, it's sauce. They're not eaten the same way."

The cyst seemed to find my distinctions absurd and shouted even louder.

Juliette and I wished we were somewhere else. The dispute kept getting worse; no appeasement was in the offing. Palamedes had recourse to a solution of which even Solomon wouldn't have dreamed: he removed the spoon from the recipient, licked it, and drank the contents of the saucer in one swig. Then he put it down, a look of disgust for the chocolate on his face.

There was a final, strangled cystic clamor:

"Soup!"

After which, the thing settled down, broken and disconsolate. She didn't touch her plate.

My wife and I were revolted. What a creep! To have forced himself to lap up a sauce he didn't like, under the pretext of teaching good manners to this poor cripple! Why couldn't he tolerate that his wife should have pleasure? I was ready to get up and prepare a whole pot of melted chocolate for this poor mammal. But I was afraid, once again, of the torturer's reaction.

From that moment on, Bernadette inspired tender sympathy in us.

After dinner we reseated the mass of our guest on the sofa, while the doctor collapsed into his chair. Juliette proposed coffee. Monsieur accepted; madame, who was pouting, emitted no sound.

My wife didn't insist, and disappeared into the kitchen.

Ten minutes later she returned with three coffees and a large cup of melted chocolate.

"Soup," she said, handing it to the thing with a kind smile.

Palamedes looked more displeased than ever, but he didn't dare protest. I felt like cheering: as usual, Juliette had had more courage than I.

The cyst gulped down the sauce, grunting with pleasure. It was repulsive, but we were thrilled. The repressed anger of her husband made us even happier.

I launched into a monologue on the role of Parmenides in the development of philosophical vocabulary. No matter how hateful, fatiguing, confused, and dry I was, my guests gave no sign of exasperation.

Little by little, I realized that they appreciated my log-orrhea, not because it interested them, but because it soothed them. Mrs. Bernardin was nothing but an enormous digestive organ. The monotonous sounds coming from my mouth brought her that marvelous calm of which the internal organs dream. Our neighbor was having an exquisite evening.

At eleven o'clock on the dot, the doctor lifted himself from his chair. If "can't" is un-American, "thank you" is un-Bernardin. On this occasion, we were the ones who wanted to thank them, since they were leaving.

They had stayed only three hours, which would have

bordered on insulting on the part of ordinary guests. But three hours spent with the Bernardins felt like twice as long. We were exhausted.

Palamedes walked into the night, pulling his matrimonial dead weight behind him. He looked like a husky sailor towing a barge.

· · ·

The next morning, we awoke with the sinking feeling we had done something wrong. We didn't know quite what, but we were sure we would suffer the consequences.

We didn't dare speak about it. Washing yesterday's dishes seemed like a blessing, just as soldiers find tedious tasks to be a calming diversion.

By afternoon, we still hadn't exchanged a word. Looking out the window, Juliette fired the first salvo in an innocent voice:

"Do you think she was already like that when he married her?"

"I was wondering the same thing. To look at her, it seems impossible she could ever have been normal. But if she was already . . . like that, why did he marry her?"

"He is a doctor."

"To marry a case like that would be pushing professional ethics a bit far."

"It happens, doesn't it?"

"You have to admit that's the least likely scenario."

"Then Mr. Bernardin is a saint."

"Some saint! Don't forget the business with the chocolate sauce."

"That's right. The soup. But you know, when you've been living with a person like that for forty-five years, you might change."

"That's probably what's made him such a rotten conversationalist. When you haven't spoken in forty-five years—"

"But she does speak."

"She is capable of expressing herself, it's true. But any conversation is impossible, as you saw. In fact, it's all coming clear: Bernardin must have come to live in this out-of-the-way spot to hide his wife. He must have become such an oaf from spending time in her company—and only her company. And he must invade our house two hours a day because what's still human in him needs human contact. We're his last hope: without us, he would sink into the amorphous state of his spouse."

"I'm beginning to understand why our predecessors left."

"It's true they were awfully evasive on the subject. . . ."

"We were the ones who didn't want to know anything. We fell in love with the House. If they had tried to tell us there were rats in the basement, we would have plugged up our ears."

"I would prefer rats."

"So would I. There are rat exterminators. There are no exterminators for neighbors."

"And with rats, you don't have to make conversation. That's the worst part: having to make conversation."

"In this case, having to keep up a monologue!"

"It's awful to think that there's no legal recourse to protect yourself from this kind of pest. In the eyes of the law, Mr. Bernardin is the ideal neighbor: he's silent—to say the least. He does nothing that can be prohibited."

"Still, he did almost break down our door."

"If only he had broken it down, we would have an excellent reason to complain to the police! Now we have nothing. If we went to the police and told them that Palamedes invades our house two hours a day, they would laugh in our faces."

"Do the police stop us from closing the door in his face?"

"Juliette, we've already discussed this."

"Let's discuss it some more. I personally am ready to stop opening the door to him."

"I'm afraid it's rooted in me. As the Bible says, 'Knock and the door shall be opened.'"

"I didn't know you were such a Christian."

"I don't know that I am. But I know that it's impossible for me not to open the door if someone is knocking on it. It's too deep. It's not only what's innate that's irreversible. There are also acquired reflexes one can't give up. Basic civic re-flexes. For example, it would be impossible for me not to say hello to people anymore, not to shake their hands any-more."

"Do you think he's coming today?"

"Want to bet on it?"

My nerves were so tense I began to laugh.

.   .   .

It was neither 3:59 nor 4:01 when the knock sounded on the door.

Juliette and I exchanged the look of the first Christians as they were being thrown to the lions.

Mr. Bernardin gave me his coat and went to take posses-sion of his armchair. In the space of an instant, I could see that he looked as if he was in a bad mood. A second later, I remembered that he looked that way every day.

I couldn't help being ironic in his presence: it was a basic self-defense mechanism. In a voice full of urbanity, I asked, "You didn't bring your charming wife?"

He looked at me thickly. I pretended not to notice.

"My wife and I adore Bernadette. The introductions have now been made. You mustn't hesitate any longer to bring her with you."

I was sincere: as long as we had to be subjected to our

torturer, I found him more colorful in the company of his better half.

Palamedes contemplated me as if I were the last of the scoundrels. He still managed to unnerve me. I began stammering, "It's true, I assure you. So what if she's . . . different? We like her very much."

The voice of a bulldog eventually responded:

"This morning she was sick!"

"Sick? The poor dear, what's wrong with her?"

He sucked in his breath to lash out a triumphal and vengeful, "Too much chocolate."

A gaze of victory: he was delighted that his wife was sick, because it gave him a wonderful occasion to accuse us.

I feigned incomprehension:

"The poor thing! She's so fragile."

Fifteen seconds of fulminations.

"No, she's not fragile. Your food is too rich."

It was clear he had decided to provoke us. I didn't take the bait.

"Not at all. You know, women are such delicate creatures . . . like porcelain from China! One emotion, and they can't digest anymore."

I was more than amused by this comparison. The neighbor, for his part, didn't find it funny: his fat face turned red. At the pinnacle of his anger, he belched:

"No, it's because of you! Because of your wife! It's the chocolate!"

Panting with rage, he lifted his chin to mark the irrefutability of his argument.

I wasn't about to be fool enough to ask his forgiveness. Sensibly, I smiled.

"Oh, it's not serious, when you're married to a great doctor. . . ."

He turned red again, shook his head, but found nothing to say.

"Dear Palamedes, tell me how you met your wife," I asked him casually, as if we were on the golf course.

He appeared so outraged by my question I thought he might leave and slam the door behind him. Alas, I was confusing my desires with reality. Finally he muttered, "At the hospital."

That was what I had suspected, but I played dumb:

"Bernadette was a nurse?"

More seconds of silent scorn.

"No."

Once again I had forgotten to structure my question properly. Following this "No," probe as I might, I could no longer obtain the slightest information on madame's origins.

He calmed down. Little by little, he became aware of his triumph. It's true we had put him in a very delicate situation;

we had forced him to show us his wife, and we had ignored his interdiction in the chocolate affair, which constituted an insult to his marital authority.

But in the end he was the winner, of course. To win out in this relentless struggle, it did no good to be the most intelligent, the most subtle; having a sense of humor and showering the other with torrents of erudition were irrelevant. To win, you had to be the heaviest, the most inert, the most oppressive, the rudest, the emptiest.

This was no doubt the word that summarized him the best: empty. Mr. Bernardin was all the more empty for being fat: because he was fat, he had more volume to contain his emptiness. So it is throughout the universe: wild strawberries, lizards, and aphorisms are dense and evoke plenitude, whereas giant gourds, cheese soufflés, and inauguration speeches are puffed up in proportion to their emptiness.

There was nothing reassuring about this thought: the power of emptiness is terrifying. It is governed by implacable laws. For example, emptiness rejects the good: it obstinately blocks its path. At the same time, emptiness asks only to be invaded by evil, as if they had an ancient relationship, as if emptiness and evil enjoyed encountering one another to relate their shared memories.

If there is a memory of water, why wouldn't there be a memory of emptiness? A memory made of xenophobia vis-à-vis the good ("I don't know you, therefore I don't love you, and I don't see why that would change") and of relations with evil ("Dear old friend, you've left so many traces of your many stays with me, make yourself at home").

It's true that someone will always say that good and evil don't exist: that is a person who has never had any dealings with real evil. Good is far less convincing than evil, but it's because their chemical structures are different.

Like gold, good is never found in a pure state in nature: it therefore doesn't seem impressive. It has the unfortunate tendency not to act; it prefers, passively, to be seen.

Evil, on the other hand, is like a gas: it's not easy to see, but it can be detected by its odor. It's most often stagnant, disbursed in a suffocating sheet; initially this aspect makes it seem inoffensive, but then suddenly you see it at work and you realize the ground it has won, the tasks it has accomplished. And by then it's all over; gas cannot be expelled.

I read in the dictionary: "Properties of gases: expandability, elasticity, compressibility, weight." One would swear this was a description of evil.

Mr. Bernardin was not evil; he was a large, empty leather bottle with a dormant and malefic gas inside. I had first thought him inert because he sat for hours doing nothing. But in fact, he only seemed to be doing nothing: in reality, he was in the process of destroying me.

. . .

At six o'clock, he left.

The next day, he arrived at four and left at six.

The day after that, arrival at four, departure at six.

And so on.

Some people have "five-to-sevens," the euphemistic name for mischievous rendezvous. I would suggest that a "four-to-six" designates the opposite.

. . .

"After all, he married a cripple."

"Is that an extenuating circumstance?"

"Imagine what his life must be like with that woman."

"I'm going to make you read *Beware of Pity.*"

"Emile, books are not the key to everything."

"Of course not. But books are also neighbors—ideal neighbors, who only come when you call them and leave as soon as you're tired of them. Consider Zweig a neighbor."

"And what does this neighbor say?"

"He says that there is a good pity and a bad pity. I'm not sure that Mr. Bernardin is practicing the good kind."

"Do we have the right to judge him?"

"With boors like him, we have every right. Does he have the right to inhabit our home two hours a day?"

"All I'm trying to say is that, initially, his desire to marry Bernadette must have been a generous impulse."

"You saw how he treated her the other night. You call that generous? Just taking care of a cripple doesn't make you a saint."

"A saint, no. But a good man."

"He is not a good man. Goodness put to bad use is not goodness."

"What would have become of her if he hadn't married her?"

"We have no idea. Who knows what she was like forty-five years ago? In any case, she couldn't have been any more unhappy without him."

"And what about him, what was he like forty-five years ago? I can't imagine that he was young and slim."

"Maybe he wasn't slim."

"But he was young, can you imagine?"

"Some people are never young."

"Well, he had to have studied medicine! Can an idiot do that?"

"I might end up believing it."

"No, it's not possible. I think it's more likely he aged very badly. It can happen. What will we be like in five years?"

"One thing is certain: you won't be like her."

Juliette laughed and began moaning, "Soup! Soup!"

.   .   .

I woke up in the middle of the night, struck by an obvious idea I hadn't yet formulated: Mr. Bernardin was the mythological nuisance.

Of course we already knew he was a nuisance. But that wasn't enough: lots of people are nuisances. Our neighbor, however, was the pure version.

I reviewed in my mind all the ancient and modern mythological figures. The possible spectrum of personalities was all there. Everyone was present, except the archetypal nuisance. There were boring types, invasive chatterboxes, exasperating seducers, neurotic women, children to be thrown from the window. Yet no one who was kin to our torturer.

Now I had been given the occasion to know someone who, except for annoying his fellow creatures, had not the slightest shadow of an activity or a reason to exist. A doctor? I had never seen him heal anyone. Placing his hand on Juliette's forehead or preventing Bernadette from gulping down chocolate sauce did not constitute a medical activity.

In truth, Mr. Bernardin was on this earth only to annoy. The proof is that he derived not an ounce of pleasure from life. I had observed him: everything was unpleasant to him. He didn't like drinking, eating, walking in nature, talking, listening, reading, looking at beautiful things—nothing. The worst of it was that he didn't even enjoy annoying me: he did it as best he could because it was his mission, but he drew no pleasure from it. He seemed to find annoying me quite annoying.

If at least he had been like those catty old women who take perverse joy in aggravating others! The thought of his happiness would have consoled me.

As it was, he poisoned his own life while poisoning mine. It was worse than a nightmare: even the most horrible dreams have an end, whereas my ordeal never finished.

Indeed, I examined the future: there was no reason for the situation to evolve. Nothing on the horizon that might resemble an outcome.

If this house had not been the House, we could have left. But we loved our clearing too much. If Moses had had a chance to dwell in the Promised Land, no Bernardin could have moved him to leave.

Another possible solution was the outcome of every human existence: death. The natural death of our neighbor. That would have been perfect. Alas, seventy years old and fat though he was, he didn't seem like a dying man. Besides, don't doctors have higher life expectancies than the average?

The final possibility was the one that Juliette kept suggesting: refuse to let him in. Naturally that's what I should have done. It was the wisdom of the law. And if I hadn't been a fearful little teacher, I would have found the strength. Alas, you don't choose to be who you are. I hadn't chosen to be a coward; it was decided for me.

Not without a certain mockery, I began thinking of it as fate. You don't teach Greek and Latin for forty years without being steeped in mythology. Thus there was, if not justice, at least a coherence to my destiny: I, a philologist, had been chosen to meet a new archetypal figure. It was like a specialist in hepatic illnesses contracting cirrhosis of the liver at the end of his life: a case of a misfortune befalling the right person.

I turned over in my bed, smiling, because I had just understood a disheartening and curious truth; namely, that meaning is the consolation of the weak.

It's true that armies of philosophers had realized this before me. But the wisdom of others has never been useful. When the cyclone hits—whether war, injustice, love, sickness, the neighbor—you're always alone, completely alone, you're a newborn and an orphan.

. . .

"How about if we bought a television?"

Juliette almost tipped over the coffeepot.

"Are you nuts?"

"Not for us, for him. That way, when he comes here, we can sit him down in front of the television and be left alone."

"Left alone, with that infernal racket?"

"You're exaggerating. It's crass, but it's not infernal."

"No, that's a very bad idea. There are two possible outcomes: either Mr. Bernardin doesn't like television, and he would be even more unhappy than before, but he still wouldn't leave. Or he likes television and he'd spend four hours, five hours, seven hours a day in our house."

"How awful. I hadn't thought of that. What if we gave them a television?"

She burst out laughing.

At that moment the telephone rang. We looked at one another in terror. In the nearly two months we'd been living in the House, we had not yet received a phone call.

Juliette stuttered, "Do you think that—"

I began raving:

"Of course it's him! Who else but him? Four to six isn't enough for him! Now it's starting at breakfast!"

"Emile, please don't answer it," my wife pleaded.

She was pale.

I swear I didn't want to pick up. But the same thing happened as when he knocked on the door: it was stronger than I was. I felt sick, I couldn't breathe. And the ringing didn't stop, thus confirming the identity of the caller.

Ashamed and at wit's end, I made a dash for the receiver

and picked it up, looking at Juliette, who had hidden her face in her hands.

Imagine how dumbfounded I was to hear, instead of the anticipated muttering, the most charming and youthful female voice in the world.

"Mr. Hazel, I'm not waking you, am I?"

I caught my breath.

"Claire!"

My wife seemed as surprised and happy as I was. Claire was the best student I'd had in forty years. She had graduated from high school the year before. We felt like her grandparents.

Little Claire explained to me that she had just obtained her driver's license. She had bought a used car that still had some spunk and was thinking of using it to come pay us a visit.

"But of course, Claire! Nothing could make us happier."

I gave her directions. She announced that she would arrive the day after the next at about three in the afternoon. I was about to rejoice when I thought of Mr. Bernardin.

Alas, the young girl was already saying good-bye. I didn't have time to suggest a different hour: quick as a sparrow, she hung up.

"She's coming the day after tomorrow," I announced in a wavering voice.

"Saturday! How wonderful! I was so afraid of not seeing her again!"

Juliette was in seventh heaven. It took some courage for me to add:

"She's arriving at three o'clock. I wanted to suggest a different time, but—"

"Oh . . ."

Her joy deflated slightly. Nonetheless, she found it in her to shrug. "Who knows? The encounter might be funny."

I wondered if she believed what she was saying.

.   .   .

Claire was a young woman of another era. I'm not saying that because she had studied Latin and Greek during her adolescence; even without that oddity, she wasn't of her time. Her face was so sweet that her peers didn't find her pretty, and she smiled so much that young people thought she was silly.

She would translate Seneca and Pindar spontaneously into elegant and subtle French: she seemed to take no account of this faculty. But her fellow students were aware of it and used this prodigious ability as an excuse to scorn her. I have often noticed that high schoolers despise intelligence.

Claire sailed above all this majestically. A true friendship was born between us. Her parents were decent people who constantly criticized her for her taste in ancient languages; they would have liked to see her choose serious studies like accounting and secretarial skills. Learning a dead language seemed the most upsetting waste of time imaginable. And to learn two of them!

One day, I had invited Claire to lunch. She must have been fifteen at the time: Juliette fell madly in love with her, and vice versa. An unusually strong bond was forged between us. Claire became the only person in the outside world who mattered to us.

Her name suited her perfectly: there emanated from her a clarity, a light that captured the eye. She was one of those exceptional beings whose mere presence is enough to bring joy.

.   .   .

Claire was eighteen years old now, but she hadn't changed: we hadn't seen her for almost a year, and nothing had altered the deep affection that united us.

She still called me "Mr. Hazel," whereas she had used Juliette's first name since their initial meeting. I didn't mind: after all, my wife was also my child, which made her closer to the girl.

Claire had been at our house only ten minutes, and we were already illuminated by her presence. It wasn't so much what she said as her manner of being. Her gaiety wore off on us. We were so happy that she hadn't forgotten us. Indifferent as we were to the outside world, she was necessary to us.

There was a knock on the door. Four o'clock already! And I had promised myself to warn her about this inopportune visit so that she would understand.

"Oh, were you expecting someone? I'll leave—"

"Claire, no! Please."

Mr. Bernardin seemed outraged that we'd had the audacity to receive a guest during the hours that now belonged exclusively to him. He muttered between his teeth when she said hello to him, armed with her exquisite smile. Juliette and I felt uncomfortable about his rudeness, as if we were responsible.

He sank into his armchair and didn't move. Claire looked at him with a kind of astonishment. She must have thought he was a friend of ours and that she therefore had to talk to him.

"What a beautiful area you live in!" she exclaimed in her charming voice.

The torturer seemed exasperated; the look on his face said, "As if I were about to speak to some ninny who dares to intrude during my hours!"

He didn't bother to open his mouth. I was aghast. Claire thought he was hard of hearing and repeated her remark louder: he looked at her as if she were a street hawker. I wanted to slap him. Instead I merely responded in his place.

"Mr. Bernardin is our neighbor. He comes here every day, from four o'clock to six o'clock."

I thought that Claire would understand the nature of these visits, that it was clear that we were being persecuted. Alas, it wasn't as apparent as all that: the young woman thought we really were friends with him. Maybe she even thought that we had invited him. A chill filled the air. An irremediable coldness. She no longer dared speak to the intruder; now she only spoke to us, but she had lost her spontaneity. As for Juliette and myself, we were so on edge that we spoke in a self-conscious manner. Our smiles rang false.

It was awful.

Claire couldn't stand it for very long. At about five o'clock, she made a move to leave. We tried to keep her; she assured us she had an engagement she couldn't cancel.

I walked her to her car. As soon as we were alone, I tried to explain the situation: "You see, it's difficult for us not to invite him in, he's our neighbor, but—"

"He's very nice. It's good company for you," she said, cutting me off, trying to help me out.

The words stuck in my throat. For the first time in my life, someone was speaking to me in a condescending manner—and it was Claire, my granddaughter, no less! She, whose favorite teacher I had been for so long, who had admired me, who had given meaning to my poor career, was now addressing me with that gentle voice reserved for old people!

She squeezed my hand with an affectionate and sad

smile, in which I read, "Come now, I can't blame you for being your age."

"You'll come back, won't you, Claire?"

"Yes, yes, Mr. Hazel. Give Juliette a kiss for me," she responded, a look of farewell in her eyes.

The vehicle disappeared into the forest. I knew that I would never see my student again.

When I returned to the living room, my wife asked me anxiously, "Will she come back?" I repeated the girl's reply: "Yes, yes."

Juliette seemed reassured. No doubt she was ignorant of a linguistic particularity: in math, a positive and a positive make a positive, whereas the word *yes* multiplied by two always equals a negative.

As for Mr. Bernardin, he seemed to understand, for I saw an expression of triumph glimmer in his lackluster eye.

.   .   .

Juliette's breath had entered a sleep mode. Finally I could relax.

I got out of bed and descended the staircase on tiptoe. It was after midnight. Without turning on the light, I sat in that cursed armchair that the torturer had appropriated for himself. I realized that by dint of bearing the weight of our neighbor, it had sunk in the middle.

I was trying to put myself in Claire's shoes. As sensitive as she was, she could only rely on appearances, and I shouldn't hold it against her.

I had made a series of errors. If I hadn't said anything about Mr. Bernardin's arrival, Claire might have understood that we were dealing with a nuisance. But I had specified that he came every day from four to six. She had therefore concluded that this imbecile was a friend.

Worse still, I had to thank her for thinking that. How could she have imagined that I would allow an intruder to invade my home? If someone had told her that her venerated professor turned out to be incapable of closing the door on such a monster, she wouldn't have believed it. She held me in too high esteem.

The worst of it was, I was getting off easy! It was all a joke, and yet I was on the verge of tears. I could hear Claire thinking out loud: "At that age, solitude is hard to take. Any company, as burdensome as it may be, is preferable to the feeling of being abandoned. Still, for a man who taught me the wisdom of the ancients, who disdained gregariousness and revered Simeon Stylites, to come to this! He had told me that he was withdrawing to the country to flee the world, like Jansen in Ypres. And here he is entertaining this rude old man every day. Well, I have to be indulgent. Old age is like a shipwreck. But I don't want to see the ship sink:

I don't have the strength for it. And I especially don't want to run into that guy again. I wonder how Juliette can stand it. . . . I won't go to see them anymore. I prefer to maintain my memory of them intact. Besides, they have a friend, they don't need me anymore."

I was trying to silence this voice. I was cursing myself. If only I'd had a chance to explain things to her, while I was walking her to her car! But I had run out of time! Why had I missed that opportunity?

For the first time in my life, I realized that I was old. And it was the look in the eyes of an affectionate young woman that had taught it to me, which made the revelation all the more terrible.

I was old, and it was my own fault. Age is no excuse today: sixty-five means nothing anymore. I could therefore only blame myself.

And with good reason. The oddity of my fault made it no less worthy of scorn. I was guilty of a particular form of weakness: I had renounced my ideal of happiness and dignity. In common language, I had allowed someone to become a pest to me. And I was accepting it for nothing, for no reason: the conventions I invoked to justify myself didn't exist.

This was an old man's behavior. I deserved to be old, because my attitudes were old.

And what about Juliette: even imagining that I had the right to make myself unhappy, how could I have taken so little account of her? I had favored the person I despised at the expense of the person I loved. And I did this despite her advice to me, which was so simple, so easy to apply: all I had to do was stop opening the door! Was it so daunting a task not to open one's door to an invader?

I hadn't seen it coming. Never would I have imagined that so trifling a weakness would entail such consequences. I couldn't hide it from myself: Claire's abandonment was stabbing me in the heart. This girl had been the only human being who with full knowledge of the facts had held me in high esteem and, in the process, had made me seem larger to myself. It's not vain to need to feel admired by someone intelligent at least once in your life. Especially if you're approaching old age and that someone is young.

And if, in addition, you have affection for your young admirer, she becomes supremely necessary: Claire was the external guarantee of my worth. For as long as she respected me, I could consider myself a person of quality.

That night I saw myself as ridiculous, mediocre, and unworthy. My entire life seemed to fall into place from this perspective.

I had been a nobody, a teacher in a rural high school. For forty years I had taught dead languages that no one cared two cents about; in the name of glorious principles, I had kept my wife a recluse, far from ordinary joys, and the little benefit I had gained from it all—the profound admiration of a gifted student—I had lost. I had read what was left of me in the eyes of youth: I was a poor old man.

In the spirit of Chekhov, I looked out the window, murmuring, "Every life is a failure. Every life is a failure." In that, my existence was ordinary, ever so ordinary, a simple slipping away.

I plunged into the hole that Mr. Bernardin had gouged in his armchair, hid my face in my hands, and cried.

.   .   .

At four in the afternoon, the instrument of my destruction arrived at my home. I withstood him as one withstands a flood. I didn't say a word to him. I hadn't shaved that morning: I spent the two hours rubbing my chin, which pricked me, strangely convinced that this beard was a product of my torturer's body.

At six o'clock, he left.

.   .   .

That night Juliette asked me when Claire would be coming back.

"She'll never come back again."

"But . . . yesterday, she told you that . . ."

"Yesterday I begged her to come back, and she responded, 'Yes, yes.' That means no."

"Why is that?"

"I read it in her eyes: she'll never come back to see us. It's my fault."

"What did you tell her?"

"Nothing."

"I don't understand."

"Yes, you do. Don't make me spell it out. You understand very well."

My wife didn't speak another word all evening. Her eyes were dead.

The next morning, she had a fever of 102 degrees. She stayed in bed. I remained at her bedside. She slept a great deal—a poor, agitated sleep.

. . .

At four o'clock, there was a knock on the door.

I was upstairs, but my hearing had become hypersensitive in recent times, like that of an animal on the alert.

A miracle happened. I felt an impulse of unprecedented strength rise within me. My rib cage swelled, my jaw contracted. Without thinking for a second, I ran downstairs, opened the door, and stared at my adversary, my eyes bulging.

His fat face registered nothing. Then my lips parted, and out poured the content of my fury. I shouted, "Get out of here! Get out of here and never come back, or I swear I'll break your face!"

Mr. Bernardin didn't react. His repertory of expressions was limited, and surprise was not one of them. His face merely clouded over; I also thought I could read a vague confusion on it that heightened my fury.

I threw myself at him, grabbed him by the collar of his coat, and with the energy of an athlete, gave him a good shake.

"Get out of here, you bloody nuisance! I never want to see you again!"

I pushed him backward like a bag of garbage. He almost fell but caught his balance just in time. He didn't look at me.

He turned around and, in his slow and heavy manner, began walking away.

Bewildered, I contemplated the departing mass. So it was that simple! I was paralyzed with feelings of joy and triumph: I had just experienced the first rage of my life, and I was drunk with it! How wrong Horace was to call it folly: on the contrary, anger was wisdom—if only it could have come to me earlier!

I slammed the door with a slap: it was sixty-five years of weakness I was slapping. Joyful and strong as a victorious general, I climbed the stairs in four bounds and landed at

Juliette's bedside, where I related my great exploit in the manner of a medieval verse chronicle:

"Do you realize! He'll never come again, never again! I promise that if he comes back, I'll break his face!"

My wife's smile was pained. She sighed.

"That's good. But Claire won't come back either."

"I'm going to call her."

"What will you tell her?"

"The truth."

"You'll admit that you let yourself be put out for two months without flinching? You'll admit that you opened the door to him, when it would have been so normal not to?"

"I'll tell her he threatened to break down our door!"

"So you'll admit that you groveled before him? That you never even spoke the words that would have liberated us? What prevented you from telling him firmly not to come anymore?"

"I'll tell her what I did today. I redeemed myself, didn't I?"

Sadly and gently, Juliette looked me in the eyes.

"Was it necessary to arrive at such an extreme? Your behavior today was excessive. You were rude and violent. You lost control of yourself. You didn't act, you exploded."

"You won't deny the efficacy of the operation! What difference does it make whether the methods were proper? Admit that Bernardin didn't deserve any better."

"Of course he didn't. But do you really intend to tell Claire about your behavior? Do you think there's reason to brag about it?"

I couldn't think of anything to say. My joy had deflated. My wife turned over in bed and murmured, "Anyway, she didn't leave us her telephone number. Or her address."

.   .   .

The next day, at four in the afternoon, there was no knock on our door.

Nor the day after that. And so on.

At 3:59 P.M., I still felt all the symptoms of anxiety: difficulty breathing, cold sweats. I was like Pavlov's dog. At four o'clock on the dot, my senses would be so heightened it was like being outside myself.

From 4:01 on, a quiver of victory would run through my body, and I would have to restrain myself from jumping up and down.

If I am referring to these events in the habitual past, it's for a reason: the conditioning lasted for days and days.

The rest of my time relaxed more quickly. I unlearned that odious feeling of expectation, but what replaced it was a far cry from happiness. The Bernardin syndrome had left its aftereffects: I rose in the morning with a profound sense of failure. I couldn't reason myself out of it—understandably so, since this sensation was on the order of the irrational.

Indeed, if I compared my situation at the moment (end of March) to that upon my arrival at the House (beginning of January), I realized that I had returned to my point of departure: the conditions had become identical. There was no longer a torturer who came to destroy my days, and these days unfolded as I had always dreamed of them, outside the world and outside time, in the deepest silence.

Of course, there was the unfortunate business with Claire: but when I came to settle here, I had never imagined nor hoped that the girl would visit us. I therefore had every reason to consider that our happiness had been restored intact, that all I had to do was dive back into it as if into a tub of warm water.

Yet I discovered that I was unable to do so. The two months of oppression by Mr. Bernardin had broken something, the nature of which was unclear to me, yet the destruction of which I experienced with painful acuteness.

For example, while Juliette certainly loved me no less than before, that climate of idyllic childhood between us was lost. She didn't reproach me in any way for my past behavior and even seemed to have forgotten about it. Yet I sensed a constant tension in her: she no longer had that marvelous capacity for letting go and for listening that I had always known in her.

We weren't unhappy, of course. We had lost only one thing, as essential as it was unknown. I reassured myself as best I could, particularly invoking the supreme healer: time. It couldn't fail to erase this bump in the road. Soon the memory would fade, soon we would find the mention of it amusing.

I so believed in this healing that I got ahead of it: already I joked about the subject, recalling certain episodes of the invasion, mimicking Palamedes's heavy bearing, or collapsing into the now depressed armchair that we persisted in calling "his" chair—without having to specify the relevant antecedent.

Juliette laughed as well. But—was it my imagination?—I had the impression her heart wasn't in it.

Sometimes I saw her stop in front of the window and stare at the neighbor's house with a look of impenetrable despair.

. . .

I will never forget the night of April 2 to 3. I have never been a sound sleeper; since the Bernardin affair, it had gotten worse. It took me hours to fall asleep. I turned over and over in bed, raving against Bernanos, who asserted that insomnia was a heightened state of abulia. Obviously, when one has faith that moves mountains, sleeping must be child's play. But when an obese doctor is your only metaphysical environment, peace of the soul becomes inaccessible.

I had been lying in bed agitated for hours. Even Juliette's hypnotic breathing didn't calm me. I was at the point of getting irritated by everything, including the silence of the forest. The sounds of the city soothe the anxiety of insomnia. Here, there was little more than the murmur of the river to connect me to life. It was a sound so slight I had to strain my ears to hear it, and this minute effort prevented my body from relaxing.

Little by little, the water began to sing more loudly. What was going on? A sudden swelling? Was the clearing about to be flooded? My muddled brain was already beginning to elaborate plans—bring the furniture upstairs, build a raft.

In a surge of awareness, I suddenly realized that there was nothing aquatic about this noise: on the contrary, it was a mechanical and lubricated buzzing, like the purring of a car.

I opened my eyes to think about it. The vehicle I was hearing wasn't moving. Yet this continuous sound was fairly distant—or at least I thought it was. It seemed to be crossing obstacles to arrive here.

My mind decided that it was a team of loggers in the process of cutting trees in the area. I believed this for five minutes, then realized how insane this hypothesis was: why would they be working at such an hour? Besides, this regular throbbing was unlike the wailing of a chain saw.

I finally got out of bed. I slipped on some old shoes and an overcoat and left the House. The noise was coming from the Bernardins'. Yet there was no light in their windows.

I concluded that they had a kind of generator to stock up on electricity. Yet it was strange that I had never heard it running before. What an idea, to wait for nighttime to turn it on! On the part of such a nuisance, though, this was no cause for surprise.

That had to be it! Our neighbor couldn't torture us anymore from four to six; to make up for it, the best he could think to do was to plug in his machine at night.

That damn Palamedes! This ridiculous operation was just his style. Because in the end, he was disturbing himself more than us with this nocturnal racket, which he must have heard ten times louder in his bed. His motto must have been simple: "Ruin your own life in the hope of ruining those of others."

I responded to him out loud, "Don't think that your new trick is bothering us, my poor friend! You should see Juliette sleeping. If I weren't an insomniac, I would never have heard that compressor of yours! But you must feel as if you're living inside a nuclear reactor right now!"

My spirits lifted, I went down to the little bridge that straddles the river and crossed over to the Bernardin property. What a beautiful night! Not a star in the sky, nothing but clouds the color of ebonite, not a breath of wind, spring still immobile in the hollow air.

As I passed round their house, I noticed a light in the garage: this must be where they had installed the generator. The noise was indeed coming from there. Our neighbor had probably forgotten to turn out the light.

I walked to the window to see the machine. Smoke filled the garage; it took me some time to figure out what was happening. The motor of the car was running.

In a quarter of a second, I understood. I rushed to the door: it was locked. I dashed to the window, which I broke with my elbow, scaled the wall, and dropped inside. I turned off the ignition and, without even glancing at the body lying on the floor, lifted the garage door.

Then I dragged Palamedes by the armpits and brought him into the fresh air.

His pulse was still beating, but he seemed to be in critical condition. His skin was gray, and a vomitlike drool covered his chin. What should I do? He was the doctor! I was the Latin and Greek teacher, not the one who could bring him back to life.

I had to call emergency. But not from his house. I was too afraid of stumbling into Bernadette. I ran to the House and called. "We'll send an ambulance," they told me, but the hospital was way out in Vauvert.

Nervously, I returned to the neighbor's side. I had the impression that his body was emitting a kind of rattle. I didn't know if that was a good sign or a bad one. I shook his arms, as if that could revive him.

I began yelling at him:

"You goddamned pest! You won't stop at anything, will you? You'll go so far as to kill yourself, just to annoy us! Well, you won't get away with it! I'm not going to let you die, do you hear? You're the biggest jerk that's ever lived!"

This didn't seem to make an impression on him. Instead, these imprecations were acting on me. I didn't deny myself the pleasure.

"What do you think? We're not at the theater here! You can't just lower the curtain when you think it's over. And if the play is so bad, it's your fault! I could be a spineless blob too: everyone has a fat motionless lump inside himself, all you have to do is let yourself go for it to appear. No one is the victim of anyone but himself. Some pretext—marrying a mental defect—to allow yourself to be a retard. You must have married her because there was already an idiot in you who recognized his other half and his ideal. From the beginning, Bernadette fit you like a glove, didn't she? I've never met such a well-matched couple. When you've found the woman of your life, you don't go and commit suicide! It's true: what would she do without you? Did you think about that before converting your garage into a gas chamber? What did you think? That we were going to take care of her? Now there's a laugh. Who do you think we are? The Salvation Army?"

I was yelling louder and louder, like madman:

"And what kind of an idea is this, for a doctor to choose such a suicide? Didn't you have a bottle of pills lying around? No, of course not, you had to choose the most disgusting method. Bad taste in everything, that's your motto. Unless . . . that's right, this was the only method that left you an escape hatch! If you had swallowed pills or hung yourself, I would never have been able to hear you. With your car, there was a chance I'd save your life. And I fell into the trap, as usual. I wonder what's stopping me from putting you back, from starting up your engine again and closing the door. Really, what's stopping me?"

If the ambulance's siren hadn't sounded at that moment, I think that, insane as I was, I would have done it.

The nurses took him away and left in a deafening roar.

I nearly begged them to take me with them too. Something inside me wasn't working anymore. I staggered to the House, where I ran into Juliette, all flustered: the wailing of the ambulance had awakened her. I told her the story bluntly. She turned pale and collapsed into a chair. She hid her faced in her hands, muttering, "What a nightmare! What a nightmare!"

Her reaction was the last straw in making me crazy.

"You mean to say, 'What a monster!' I forbid you to feel sorry for him! Don't you see that he was acting out with the sole intention of driving us nuts?"

"Come on, Emile . . ."

"It's as if you didn't know him! And I walked into his trap like a dope. Now he'll be able to claim martyrdom! I should have let him die, of course. Not only did I blow a wonderful opportunity to get rid of him, but in addition, we'll be forced to be good Samaritans toward him from now on, we'll have him on our backs all the time."

Juliette stared at me in horror. For the first time in sixty years, she spoke to me curtly:

"Do you realize what you're saying? You're the monster! How can you believe such an abomination? If you hadn't had insomnia, you would never have heard him, and he would be dead as we speak. You're talking like a murderer, a real murderer."

"A murderer! You forget that I saved his life."

"It was your duty! Once you knew what was happening, it was your duty. If you had let him die, you would have been a murderer. And what you just said is ignoble."

If she only knew that I had almost put him back in his gas chamber! I thought—but I was no longer terribly pleased with my thinking.

"And Bernadette?" she added, softly.

"I didn't see her. In my opinion, she knows nothing about what happened."

"Do we have to tell her?"

"Do you think she'd understand? Right now, I bet she's sleeping, which is what's best for her."

"Tomorrow she'll see he's not there when she wakes up, and she'll panic."

"Let's wait until tomorrow."

"You want us to go back to bed and fall asleep! As if we could sleep after this!"

"What's your suggestion?"

"That you go to the hospital, and I go to see her."

"Are you crazy? She's five times your size. She could kill you!"

"She's harmless."

"I would be too afraid for you. I'll go. They don't need me at the hospital."

"I'll come with you."

"No. Someone has to stay at the House. I gave our telephone number to the ambulance driver."

"Then go ahead and stay with her. Someone has to be near her when she wakes, so that she doesn't have time to worry."

"I think we're being awfully kind to these people."

"Emile, it's the least we can do! If you don't go, I'll go myself."

I sighed. It's not always easy having a wife with a heart of gold. But she was right about one thing: I wouldn't have been able to fall asleep.

. . .

I took a flashlight and kissed my wife like a soldier heading for the front.

The door that connected the garage to the interior of their house wasn't bolted. The glow of my flashlight illuminated a kitchen as I entered. A fetid smell filled my lungs: I didn't dare imagine what the Bernardins had eaten. Peels littered the floor. I made no attempt to identify what they were; I had only one thing in mind: to leave this dump as soon as possible and find some breathable air.

I opened the door to the kitchen and closed it behind me to prevent the musty smell from spreading. No luck: an identical stench prevailed in the living room. It was putrid. How could human beings live in this? In particular, how could a doctor so defy the most elementary rules of hygiene?

My nose analyzed the components of this bouquet: a layer of old onions, of spoiled grease, the sweat of an old goat, and, strangest and most unpleasant of all, a powerful whiff of oxidized metal. This last smell was the worst, because it suggested nothing human, animal, or vegetable: I had never smelled anything so unhealthy.

I found a switch and turned on the light: what I saw made me want to giggle. When bad taste reaches such a degree, that is all you can do. I was nonetheless astonished: in general, kitsch furnishing tends toward an excess of comfort and coziness—what Germans call *gemütlich*. Here, you would have thought you were in a streetcar decorated by a janitor: it was squalid, cold, and ridiculous all at once.

No paintings on the walls, except for Palamedes's medical diploma, framed grandiloquently, like a portrait of Stalin. That a namesake for Proust's Baron de Charlus—whose first name was indeed Palamedes—could stretch the meaning of ugliness and vulgarity to such an extreme was the limit!

I was about to break into laughter when I recalled my mission. I climbed to the second floor. A layer of sticky dust covered the stairs. When I reached the top, I stood still and pricked up my ears. I seemed to perceive a kind of groan.

I was tempted to run. This harsh sound couldn't be related to a snore: what I heard was reminiscent of the sexual pleasure of an animal. I rejected this possibility: it was too unpleasant to consider.

The first door in the hallway opened onto a junk room. The second door as well. The last, onto a bathroom. I had to face the facts: one of the junk rooms was a bedroom.

I returned to the first door and opened it: the groan informed me I was in the right place. Terrified, I entered Bernadette's sanctuary. My flashlight hit on unidentifiable objects, then, at the end of its search, stumbled over a pallet covered with a moving mass.

There she was. Her eyes were closed: I was comforted to realize that the moaning sound corresponded to the rhythmic breath of slumber. She was sleeping.

I flipped the switch: a hideous chandelier spread a surgical block of light. Mrs. Bernardin was unperturbed. If her own decibels didn't wake her, after all, nothing could.

The couple slept in separate rooms. I concluded that Palamedes occupied the other junk room. There was no place for another body—and especially not for another large body—on the pile of rags that served as a bed for the cyst.

For certain reasons, the nature of which I prefer not to explore, I felt relieved at the idea that they didn't sleep together. It was fortunate as well: thanks to this nocturnal separation, Bernadette was unaware of the suicide attempt and was gaining several extra hours of rest.

I sat down next to her on a synthetic footrest and began watching her. Opposite me, a large clock indicated four in the morning: I smiled at the thought that I was invading their house at the hour diametrically opposite the one at which mine had been invaded. I then realized that there

were three clocks and an alarm clock in this room: they all
indicated the same hour to the second. Thinking back on
the living room, the stairs, and the hallway, I realized that
they too were studded with clocks: no doubt they were all
perfectly punctual, like those in this room.

This detail, already surprising in and of itself, was especially striking amid such disorder: their home was dirty, the
air was stagnant, the rooms were bursting with cardboard
boxes filled with disgusting old things, and yet, at the heart
of this sinister abandon, someone was making sure that time
was omnipresent and of unholy precision.

I was beginning to understand why Palamedes always arrived precisely on the hour. If he had wanted to furnish himself with a suicidal interior, he couldn't have done any
better: this house—at once horrible, heartbreaking, nox-
ious, grotesque, filthy, and uncomfortable—and finally and
especially this proliferation of clocks, adjusted to the hun-
dredth of a second, reminded you five times per room that
time was crushing down on you. Hell must be like this.

A yelp from Mrs. Bernardin brought my attention around
to her. Was she asthmatic, to produce such a rattle? The
calm of her pose suggested otherwise. I observed her: cycli-
cally, her enormous chest lifted like a hot-air balloon that,
when it reached maximum inflation, collapsed in a single
and sudden depression, provoking this monstrous sigh each

time. There was no cause for alarm; it was a phenomenon explicable by the laws of physics.

Upon reflection, I realized I had never seen anyone sleep with so much consciousness: it seemed she applied herself to it. When I examined what served as her face, I was stupefied to discover a true sensual pleasure. I remembered that, from the corridor, I had compared this noise to the orgasm of a beast: this sexual suspicion was wrong, but Bernadette did experience pleasure. Sleep for her was orgasmic.

I was curiously moved. There was something touching in the delectation of this enormous heap. I surprised myself thinking that she was far superior to her husband: her life was not absurd, since she had pleasure. She liked to sleep, she liked to eat. It didn't matter whether these activities were noble or not: pleasure elevates, whatever its source.

Palamedes liked nothing. I had never seen him sleep, but there was every reason to think that he did it with disgust, as he did everything else. For the first time, I realized that we had gotten things reversed: he wasn't the one to pity for having spent forty-five years with her. She was. I wondered if she had feelings. How would she take the news of the suicide attempt? Would she understand the meaning of this word?

I murmured with a kind of affection, "If he had died, who would have watched out for you? Can you use your hands—

well, your tentacles? How do you spend your days? You can't eat and sleep nonstop. Do you know who you remind me of? Of Regina, my grandmother's dog. I adored her when I was a child. She was an old, old animal who divided her life between sleep and food. She woke up only to eat and went back to sleep the second she had finished. You had to drag her to move her ten feet. Is your schedule just like Regina's?"

I hadn't thought about that fat dog in at least fifty years. I smiled at the memory.

"People used to make fun of her, but I loved her. I would watch her: she had decided to live only for pleasure. When she ate, her tail wagged. When she slept, she was like you: her flesh was brimming with pleasure. Deep down, you and she are both philosophers."

To my eyes, there was nothing insulting about comparing someone to an animal. Anyone who has read the Greeks and Romans knows how highly we should regard the animal kingdom.

I contemplated Mrs. Bernardin tenderly. Watching her sleep, padded in her flesh, was the most soothing of sights. I found myself hoping she would never wake up.

An unlikely thing happened: I, who was predisposed to insomnia, in particular that night, fell asleep on the synthetic pouf, rocked by Bernadette's rattle.

. . .

I awoke with a start. From the depths of her pallet, the cyst hardly dared look at me; she expressed her intimidation by tiny grunts.

An armada of clocks broadcast that it was eight o'clock in the morning. I remembered my mission. Embarrassed, I began gently:

"Bernadette . . . your husband had a little accident. He's in the hospital. Don't be afraid, he's out of danger."

Mrs. Bernardin didn't react. She continued staring at me. I felt it was necessary to explain.

"He tried to commit suicide. I stopped him. Do you understand?"

I never knew whether she had understood. She rested her head on the pallet. A poet would have said she had a pensive air; in reality, she had no expression at all.

Tired, discouraged, and perplexed, I left. I had performed my duty. Indeed, what more could I have done?

Upon exiting the neighbor's home, I was struck by the purity of the air. It dazzled me more than the light. How had I managed to breathe in that nauseating hovel? I was reminded how good it was to be among the living.

At the House, Juliette ran into my arms.

"Emile, I was so afraid!"

"Any news from the hospital?"

"Yes, he's okay. He'll be sent home the day after tomorrow. When the doctors questioned him about the motive for his action, he didn't answer."

"I would have been surprised if he had!"

"They asked him if he was going to try it again, and he said no."

"We'll see. Do they know he's a doctor himself?"

"I have no idea. Why? What difference does it make?"

"It's just that it seems to me that the suicide of a doctor would draw people's attention."

"More than someone else's?"

"Maybe. In a sense, it's a violation of the Hippocratic oath."

"Tell me how Bernadette responded."

I retraced the last hours. I took delight in describing the interior of the Bernardin household. Juliette screamed with revulsion and giggled almost simultaneously.

"Do you think we have to take care of her?" she asked.

"I don't know. We might do her more harm than good."

"We have to feed her at least. We'll bring her soup."

"Melted chocolate?"

"For dessert. Along with a large pot of vegetable soup. I imagine she eats quite a lot."

"It'll be a holiday for her. In my opinion, she'll spend two marvelous days without her husband."

"Who knows? Maybe she loves him."

I said nothing, but it seemed to me impossible to love Palamedes.

·   ·   ·

In Mauves, we bought almost every vegetable available at the grocery store. When we returned from the village, we prepared a potful of soup. I watched this flood boil in the depths of the stewpan, spitting up leeks and celery to the surface: it looked like a tempest at sea, a waltz of algae and plankton. I imagined the future of this oceanic broth in the intestines of the cyst: a veritable whale's lunch, both in nature and quantity.

Toward noon Juliette and I carried a tray to the other side of the river. The two of us could barely carry the load: a potful of soup and a small dish of chocolate sauce. My wife laughed in disgust upon entering the kitchen.

"It's worse than you described."

"The smell, or the way it looks?"

"Everything!"

No one was downstairs. We went to the second floor. Mrs. Bernardin had not left her pallet. She wasn't sleeping, she wasn't doing anything: her serenity took the place of an occupation. Juliette began speaking effusively with surprising sincerity:

"Bernadette, I've been thinking about you a great deal. Your courage is admirable. The hospital called: your husband is fine, and will be home the day after tomorrow."

We never knew whether she had understood or even listened: she tolerated my wife's kiss, her gaze fixed on the little dish. Her sense of smell identified the contents immediately. She who was so calm began gurgling, casting her tentacles toward the delicacy.

"That's right, we made two different soups for you. You have to start with the large one; the other is dessert."

The lady would hear nothing of it. After all, what difference did the order of the dishes make? Juliette gave her the sauce dish: the neighbor was jumping out of her skin, salivating noisily. Her tentacles closed around the treasure, which she held up to her buccal orifice. She drank the contents in one gulp, grunting like a cross between a warthog and a sperm whale.

The sight of this pleasure was both heartening and repellent: a corner of my wife's mouth smiled, while the other side was trying not to vomit.

The cyst laid down the empty dish: she had licked the sides, so that it was immaculate. Her long tongue emerged again to clean the chin and the mustache. Something moving then happened: Mrs. Bernardin heaved a sigh—an interminable sigh of well-being, with a note of disappointment because it was over.

Juliette poured the vegetable soup into a bowl and handed it to her. Bernadette sniffed with curiosity, lapped up a bit, and seemed to find our broth agreeable. She swallowed it, making sounds like a drain.

"I should have strained the soup," said my wife, seeing that bits of greenery hadn't entered the orifice and remained stuck to her chin, like seaweed on a beach.

Then the neighbor emitted a Melvillian burp and fell back onto the pallet. In the space of a second, I thought I could read in her eyes the expression of a queen mother telling her subjects, "Thank you, good subjects, you may disperse."

She closed her eyes and instantly fell asleep. The groaning of her slumber combined with a digestive process as noisy as a washing machine.

"Let's leave the pot and go," I whispered, both touched and repulsed.

. . .

The next day, Juliette strained the soup.

. . .

For two days in a row, we found the pot empty and madame full. She didn't leave her room, except for her personal business—which we were relieved to find we did not have to help her with.

"If you want my opinion, these are the happiest days of Bernadette's life."

"Do you think so?" asked my wife.

"Yes. First of all, your cooking is certainly better than her husband's, and since food is the mainstay of her existence, this change is a marvelous revolution for her. But the best thing is that we're leaving her in peace. I'm convinced that Palamedes forces her to get up and go downstairs to the living room for no reason."

"Why would he do that?"

"To pester her. That's his obsession in life."

"Maybe also to wash her. Or to change her."

I laughed at the thought of Mrs. Bernardin's nightshirt: a titanic polyester dress printed with wildflowers, its collar made of village lace.

"Don't you think we should give her a bath?" suggested Juliette.

In a flash I imagined a bathtub full of white flesh.

"I propose we leave that task to her husband."

.   .   .

The day after the next, the hospital called: they were giving us the green light to collect the other half of the couple.

"I'll go alone. You have the soup to prepare."

As I was driving, I found myself incensed at having to pick him up. "We should leave him there," I thought.

In the office, I was asked to sign a stack of incomprehensible papers. Mr. Bernardin, undaunted, was waiting for me in a corridor. The universal bore was slouched in his chair. When he saw me, he assumed the dissatisfied air he always had with me. He said nothing, raised the mass of his body, and followed me. I noticed that the nurses hadn't washed his clothes, which still bore traces of vomit.

During the car ride, he didn't speak a word. That was fine with me. I told him we had fed his wife in his absence. He didn't react to anything, didn't look at anything; I wondered if his gas poisoning hadn't ravaged the few mental faculties he had left.

The weather was gorgeous that day: a textbook early April, with flowers light as Maeterlinck heroines. I considered that if I had emerged from a suicide attempt, such a delicious spring would have swelled my heart to the point of tears: this landscape saturated in rebirth would have seemed linked to my own resurrection. I would have felt deeply reconciled with the world I had wished to leave behind.

Apparently, Palamedes was impermeable to all that. I had never seen him so sunk into himself.

I stopped the car in front of his door. As I was leaving, I asked him if he needed any help.

"No," he responded in his grouchy voice.

He had thus preserved the use of speech—if such parsimonious usage can be considered use.

The question that was on the tip of my tongue escaped from my mouth:

"Do you know that I was the one who saved your life?"

For the first time, Mr. Bernardin was terrifyingly eloquent. Not that he enriched his vocabulary, but he exploited his silence and his gaze like an established orator. He fixed his outraged eyes on mine, was silent to the limit of the tolerable, and when the length of my suspended breath seemed sufficient to him, simply said, "Yes."

Then he turned and entered his home.

Frozen, I returned to the House. Juliette asked me how he was. I answered, "The same."

"I prepared even more soup than yesterday. I left it out in their living room."

"That was nice of you, but in the future, let them fend for themselves."

"You don't think he would like it if I cooked instead of him?"

"Juliette, you don't seem to understand: he doesn't like anything!"

.   .   .

The next morning, the pot was perched in front of our door; the contents were untouched.

We were being dismissed.

. . .

The weeks slipped past. Contrary to what I had feared, the neighbor did not show up at our house even once. He barely stuck his nose outdoors. Yet the sweetness of the month of April was provocative: Juliette and I would spend hours in the garden, eating lunch and even breakfast there. We would take long walks in the forest, where the birds performed *Le Sacre du printemps* for us, revised and arranged by Janáček.

Palamedes only left the house to drive to the village. His errands were the sole social element of his existence.

May arrived, the daintiest of months—I say that without irony: the poor city dweller that I have always been delighted unabashedly in the thousand fopperies of nature. No spectacle was too commonplace. The simpering of the lily of the valley plunged me into true emotional upheaval.

I told my wife the legend of the lilac forest, inspired as I was by the blue-and-white combustion of the garden. Juliette insisted she had never heard such a beautiful story; that I should tell it to her every day.

Mr. and Mrs. Bernardin must have been insensitive to this riot of color: they were never seen in their yard. Their windows were always closed, as if they were afraid to dilute their precious stench.

"What's the point of living in the country?" said Juliette.

"Don't forget that he must have chosen to live here to hide his wife. Palamedes couldn't care less about flowers."

"And what about her? I'm sure she likes them and would be delighted to see them."

"He's ashamed of her, he doesn't want her to be seen."

"But we already know what she looks like! No one could see her but us."

"He's not exactly obsessed with Bernadette's happiness."

"What a bastard! Sequestering that unhappy woman! Are we going to put up with that?"

"What would you like us to do? There's nothing illegal about it."

"What if we went to get her and brought her outside, would that be illegal?"

"You saw how she walks."

"Not to walk. We'll put her in the garden so she can see the flowers, so she can breathe the air."

"He'd never agree to that."

"We won't ask him! We'll catch him off guard, we'll go to his house and say, 'We've come to get Bernadette to spend the afternoon with us on our patio.' What can we lose?"

Though unenthusiastic, I had to agree she was right. After lunch, we went to knock on their door (things were becoming reversed, I thought). No one opened it. I began banging like a savage, following Palamedes's example that winter, but I didn't have his strength. There was no reaction.

"And to think that I felt obliged to open for him!" I exclaimed to myself, my fists on fire.

Juliette finally took it upon herself to enter. The courage of this sixty-five-year-old girl astounded me. I followed her. The mustiness of the nightmarish interior had gotten even worse.

Mr. Bernardin was sprawled in a chair in the living room, surrounded by clocks. He looked at us with exasperation and wariness; he seemed to think we were mighty invasive neighbors—which took the cake, coming from him.

Without saying a word, as if he didn't exist, we went upstairs. The cyst was lying on her pallet, wearing a pink nightshirt with daisies.

Juliette kissed her on the cheek:

"We're taking you to the garden, Bernadette! You'll see how nice it is outside."

Mrs. Bernardin allowed herself to be towed in good grace: we each held a hand. She descended the steps one by one, like a two-year-old child. We walked past Palamedes without explaining where we were going—without even looking at him.

Since there was no chair fit to accommodate her, I laid a sheet and cushions on the grass. We deposited our neighbor onto it; lying on her belly, she contemplated the garden with an expression close to astonishment. Her right tentacle caressed the small white daisies, carrying one to a centimeter from her eyes to examine it.

"I think she's nearsighted," I said.

"Do you realize that without us, this woman would never have seen a daisy up close?" said Juliette, indignant.

Bernadette submitted the novelty to each of her senses: after looking at the plant, she sniffed it, listened to it, rubbed it against her forehead, and finally, chewed and swallowed it.

I went into raptures:

"Her procedure is incontestably scientific! This person is intelligent!"

As if to disprove my words, the creature began to cough in a repulsive fashion until the daisy reemerged: this food didn't suit her.

At the cost of a heartbreaking effort, she turned over; then she let herself fall back, panting and inert. Her eyes fixed on the blue of the sky and stopped moving. There was no doubt about it: she was happy. It was quite a change from the dark ceiling of her room.

At about four o'clock, Juliette went to fetch tea and cookies. She drew near the recumbent figure and slipped pieces of shortbread into the buccal orifice. Our guest made clucking sounds: she liked that.

To our amazement, we heard a scream: "She can't eat that!"

It was Palamedes, who had been spying on us from behind the window of his living room for hours, waiting for us to do something "wrong." At the sight of our crime, he had emerged onto his doorstep to restore order.

Regally, my wife recovered her cool and continued to feed the cyst, as if nothing had happened. My heart was in my boots: what if we were to come to blows? He was much stronger than we were.

But Juliette's maneuver intimidated him. Disconcerted, he stood ten minutes on the doorstep contemplating our disobedience. After which, to exit gracefully, he cried a second time, "She can't eat that!"

He disappeared into his warehouse of clocks.

At nightfall, we guided Mrs. Bernardin to her home. We entered without knocking. Her husband greeted us with, "And if she's sick, it will be your fault!"

"You'd like that, wouldn't you, if your wife were sick?" Juliette said.

We reinstalled her on her pallet. She seemed exhausted from so much emotion.

.   .   .

We should have expected it: the next day, he locked all the doors to his house.

"He's sequestering his wife, Emile! How about if we call the police?"

"Unfortunately, there's still nothing illegal about his actions."

"Even if we specify that he attempted to commit suicide?"

"They won't arrest him for that."

"What about if he were in the process of killing his wife?"

"We have no reason to suspect that."

"What do you mean? Do you realize he's locked her up simply because she nibbled some cookies?"

"Maybe he wants her to lose weight."

"What good would losing weight do her with the life she leads? And anyway, hasn't he looked at himself?"

"We know very well what this is all about. Mr. Bernardin experiences no pleasure in life: he can't stand for his wife not to be like him. Yesterday, he saw her go into ecstasy over a daisy, swoon at the blue of the sky, then belch with delight after eating cookies. It's more than he can bear."

"And you don't find that disgusting, preventing a poor old mentally deficient woman from enjoying life?"

"Of course I do, Juliette! That's not the problem: so long as his actions are legal, there's nothing we can do."

"Why don't I just break a window and go get Bernadette?"

"In that case, he'd be the one in a position to call the police. How would that help our cause?"

"We really can't react?"

"I'll tell you something awful: yesterday, in our desire to bring her a moment of beauty, we harmed that poor creature. She's locked up now, and it's our fault. I think it would be best to cut her losses. The more we want to help her, the more we'll worsen her fate."

· · ·

The argument carried. Juliette no longer spoke of saving the cyst. But it was clear she was obsessed with the matter. Spring changed nothing: each day was sweeter than the one before. I ended up hoping for rain: the fine weather was making my wife sad. As we were walking, she would say, "She can't see these red currants. She can't see these tender green leaves."

No need to specify to whom "she" referred. The slightest bud became a piece of evidence and added to a charge that I could sense was directed against me and not our neighbor.

One morning, I exploded:

"Deep down you blame me for having prevented his suicide!"

She responded in a low, firm voice, "No, not at all. You had to stop him."

I was glad she was so convinced of this. I myself wasn't so sure. I rued the day I had saved him. I considered myself one hundred percent in the wrong.

Anyway, wasn't he the first to hold it against me? He had expressed this with rare eloquence the day I brought him back from the hospital.

The worst of it was that now I agreed with him. I put myself in his shoes and arrived at this horrifying conclusion: he was absolutely right to want to die.

Because life, for him, must have been hell, and I was finally beginning to understand that it wasn't his fault. He hadn't chosen for his five senses to be frigid: he was born that way.

I tried to imagine his fate: to feel nothing at the sight of the forest's beauty, at the sound of arias that are dazzling to others, at the scent of a tuberous plant. Not to enjoy eating or drinking, touching or being touched. That meant that no art had ever moved him. And that he knew nothing of sexual desire.

Some people are stupid enough to use the expression "blinded by one's senses." Have they ever thought about the blindness of those who aren't illuminated by their senses?

I felt a shiver run through me: how empty Mr. Bernardin's life was! If you consider that the senses are the doors to intelligence, to the soul, and to the heart, what was left for him?

Even mysticism is learned through pleasure. Not necessarily through the experience of pleasure, but definitely through the notion of it: monks who abstain from the life of the flesh at least have a sense of what they are deprived of. And lacking something teaches as much, if not more, than having an abundance. But Palamedes didn't suffer any lack; if you love nothing, you lack nothing.

Haven't the lives of saints proven that religious ecstasy is rapturous? If absolute abstinence were a trance state, we would know it.

Alas, it wasn't necessary to look to such extremes to surmise the neighbor's emptiness: not the grandiose void described by Hugo but a shabby, sordid, ridiculous, and pitiful emptiness. The grumpy emptiness of a poor nobody.

A poor nobody who, last but not least, had never loved anyone, nor dreamed that love was possible. Of course, I didn't want to get cheaply sentimental: people can live without loving—one need only look at the common fate of man to be convinced of it. Except that men who are strangers to love all have something else: cards, poker, football, crossword puzzles—anything, no matter what, so long as they can forget themselves.

But Mr. Bernardin had nothing. He was imprisoned in himself. There was no window in his cell. And what a cell! The worst kind: that of an obese old brute.

Suddenly, I understood his obsession with clocks: unlike the living, Palamedes blessed the passing of time. The only light in the depths of his prison was his death: the twenty-five clocks in his house were measuring the slow, steady pace that was leading him there. After his death, he would no longer be present at his absence, he would no longer have flesh to contain his void; he would become emptiness instead of living it.

One night, a surge of will had prompted this man to escape his penitentiary: it had taken courage to make this decision. And I, wretched warder that I was, had caught the poor guy as he was making his getaway. Proud as a stool pigeon, I had returned him to his prison.

It was all coming clear: from the start, his behavior had been that of a convict. In the beginning, when he imposed on me two hours a day, he was the convict with nothing better to do than invade another's cell. His gluttony, despite his distaste for food, was typical of those who are suffering supreme boredom. His sadism toward his wife was also typical of the incarcerated: the pathetic need to impose their own suffering on a victim. His slovenliness, his poor hygiene, his physical decline, were common to those condemned to life in prison.

It was all so clear! Why hadn't I seen it sooner?

. . .

One night I awoke with a start with this unavowable thought: "Why doesn't he try again? They say those who attempt suicide are recidivists. What is he waiting for?"

Perhaps he was afraid I would interfere again. How could

I signal to him that this time, I wouldn't throw a wrench in the works?

I thought again about the means he had chosen for his suicide: why exhaust fumes? Was it in the hope of being saved? No, the chances were too slim. He must have chosen it out of masochism: yet another example of prisonerlike behavior. Perhaps this man, who was suffocating inside himself, wanted to die of asphyxiation. It would have been a thousand times simpler and less painful for him to inject himself with poison, but isn't it possible that, like all suicides, he felt the need to leave a message? Some leave letters, which he would have been incapable of writing. His chosen signature would have been his barbarous death, which implicitly contained his epitaph: "I am dying as I lived."

On the night of April 2, without my cursed insomnia, Mr. Bernardin would have found salvation. Now it was early June. An absurd idea popped into my head: what if I were to send him a note? "Dear Palamedes, now I understand. You can try it again, I won't disturb you." I buried my mouth in the pillow so as not to laugh out loud.

Then this idea began to seem less outrageous to me. I even began envisioning it seriously. At first glance, such a letter seemed cynical and criminal, but upon further reflection, it was what my neighbor needed. I had to help him.

Suddenly I couldn't wait any longer. This missive was of the utmost importance! I got up, went down to the living room, took a sheet of paper, and jotted down the two liberating phrases. I crossed the bridge and slipped the note beneath the Bernardins' door.

A feeling of bliss and relief washed over me. I had performed my duty. I went back to bed and fell asleep with the idyllic impression of having been the messenger of divine love. Seraphs were singing in my head.

· · ·

When I awoke the next day, it seemed to me I had dreamed it all. Little by little, I became aware of the reality of my act: I had truly written that vile letter, and had gone so far as to slide it under his door! I had lost my mind.

As Juliette watched in surprise, I grabbed her tweezers and ran outside. Lying on the ground before the neighbor's door, I slid the tweezers into the crack, blindly, to recuperate the note. My efforts bore no fruit: the paper was too far inside—or else Palamedes had already read it.

Horrified, I returned home.

"Can you tell me why you were sprawled out in front of their door with my tweezers?"

"I slipped him a letter last night, and now I regret it. But I couldn't get it back."

"What did you write?"

I didn't have the courage to confess the truth.

"Insults. Things like: 'You're disgusting to lock up your wife,' and so on."

Juliette's eyes sparkled.

"Bravo. I'm glad you didn't get it back. I'm proud of you."

She took me in her arms.

. . .

My day was spent in self-loathing. That night I went to bed early and fell asleep as if trying to get away from myself. At two in the morning, I woke up: impossible to get back to sleep.

I then understood a terrible thing: there were two Emile Hazels. Indeed, during this period of insomnia, I considered myself right to have written that letter. I no longer felt the slightest shame. On the contrary, I was pleased with my action.

Was I a new Dr. Jeykll? I rejected this overly Gothic hypothesis. Yet I realized that nighttime had a tremendous influence on me. My nocturnal ideas always envisaged the worst and left no room for possibilities such as improvement, hope, or even benign indifference. During my nights of insomnia, everything was tragic, everything was my fault!

A singular question then arose: which of the two Emile Hazels was right? The daytime one, the slightly cowardly one who withdrew from the game before he could lose? Or the nocturnal one, disgusted with life, a rebel ready to perform the most daring actions to help others live—or die?

I resolved to wait until the next day to figure it out. In the morning, my insomniac ruminations seemed wrong. Once again I was ready for any compromise.

· · ·

Several days later, I was reassured. Mr. Bernardin was alive and well, and I considered myself an idiot for having imagined that my letter would influence him.

I pictured Palamedes collecting my note, reading it, and shaking his head with the scorn he had reserved for me from the beginning. I sighed with relief.

I finally understood the myth of Penelope, whose precepts I was far from the first to experience: do we not all destroy by night the personas we compose for ourselves by day, and vice versa? The wife of Ulysses played her suitors' game by weaving her tapestry by day and becoming the haughty heroine of negation by night. Light favored the limp comedy of civility; darkness left humans with a destructive rage.

· · ·

"In your opinion, Juliette, why doesn't he try to commit suicide again? They say suicidal people are recidivists. So why doesn't he try again?"

"I don't know. I imagine he learned his lesson."

"What lesson?"

"That we won't let him get away with it."

"As if we were in a position to watch him!"

"Maybe he's recovered a taste for life."

"Does he seem like he has?"

"How can we know?"

"Look at him."

"I can't: he locks himself up at home."

"Precisely. He lives in an earthly paradise, it's the prettiest springtime in the world, and he stays inside."

"Some people aren't sensitive to such things."

"And what is he sensitive to, in your opinion?"

"To clocks." She smiled.

"That's true. He loves clocks the way Lady Death likes her scythe. Let me restate my question then: what is he waiting for, for his second suicide attempt?"

"It sounds like you're hoping for it."

"No. I'm only trying to understand him."

"All I can say is this, Emile: it seems to me that even if you want to die, to kill yourself must be terrifying. I once read the memoirs of a parachutist: he said that it was the second leap into the void that scared him the most."

"So in your opinion, he's not making a second attempt because he's afraid?"

"That would be human, wouldn't it?"

"In that case, do you realize the despair this poor guy must feel? He wants to die, and he can't find the courage to kill himself."

"That's what I thought: you want him to try again!"

"Juliette, what I want is irrelevant. What counts is what he wants."

"And you want to help him, basically?"

"No!"

"Then why are you talking to me about it?"

"So that you'll stop judging his fate from your own perspective. It's been drummed into your head that life has value."

"Even if it hadn't been drummed into my head, I would think so. I love living."

"Are you incapable of conceiving that there are people who don't love living?"

"Are you incapable of conceiving that there are people who can change their minds? He can learn to love life."

"At seventy years old?"

"It's never too late."

"You're an incorrigible optimist."

"You said that the suicidal are recidivists. Don't you think that all human beings are recidivists?"

"'Human beings are recidivists': very poetic, but I don't understand."

"A human being doesn't do anything once. If you do one thing one day, it's because it's in your nature. We all spend our time reproducing the same acts. Suicide is only one particular case. Assassins go back to killing, lovers fall in love again."

"I don't know if that's true."

"I believe it."

"Then you believe that he's going to try to commit suicide again?"

"It was you I was thinking of, Emile. You saved him. You won't be happy to save him just once."

"How am I going to save him?"

"I don't know, that's not my business," she said, adding with a radiant smile, "You're the savior, not me."

Ever since I had lied to her about the letter full of insults, Juliette looked at me like I was a kind of messiah. It was maddening.

"Deep down, Juliette, we're fools. Why go to so much trouble to help a man we despise? Even Christians don't do as much."

"We love Bernadette. So long as Palamedes isn't well, he'll take revenge on his wife. The only way to help that poor creature is to save her husband."

"Save him from what?"

.   .   .

The burst of broom came to an end. Now it was the wisteria's turn.

To be unhappy in June is as inconvenient as being happy while listening to Schubert. That's what makes this month intolerable: for thirty days you feel as if the slightest moodiness is rude. Nothing is worse than forced happiness.

The wisteria aggravates the situation. What could be more heartrending than a wisteria in bloom? Those blue bunches crying the length of the curved woody vines get the better of my scant self-possession and transform me into a ridiculous, overemotional Lamartinian. When I was little, I would spend Sundays at my grandmother's. A wisteria climbed the wall of her house. In June, this blue rain tore at my heart, and already I was at a loss to understand myself: I would burst into tears, aware of the absurdity of my reaction.

The antidote for wisteria is asparagus, another glory of the month of June. I've noticed that it's impossible to feel sad while eating it. The problem is that you can't eat it twenty-four hours a day.

It would have taken quite a few bunches of asparagus that early June to dispel my anxieties. At night, I contemplated Juliette the way Christ on the Mount of Olives watched his sleeping disciple: she had been blessed with calmness and confidence at birth, and counted on me to sustain these two gifts that I myself had been refused.

The insomnia became more bearable once I got out of

bed. I would go into the garden. The freshness of the night made me stagger, the wisteria knocked me out. Well-bred Japanese send one another letters in which they write only about the flowers of the moment; others make fun of this ritual, said to be superficial. If I were Japanese, I would probably be a great letter writer: this formalism would allow me to express the sentiments of a sappy young girl without anyone even noticing.

The equation didn't compute: Juliette was demanding that I save Mr. Bernardin. Yet my personal conviction was that only death could release him from his prison. But my wife didn't want him to die. And even if she had wanted it, he no longer seemed inclined to commit suicide.

As I gazed at the wisteria, I made a decision that struck me as awful: from now on, I would accept that Juliette might not understand me.

. . .

This resolution had repercussions from the very next morning. When I saw the neighbor's car returning from the village, I rushed to meet it.

"Palamedes, I must speak to you."

Without a word, he slipped the keys into the lock of his trunk but didn't open it. He remained standing, motionless next to the car.

"Did you get my letter?"

Fifteen seconds of silence.

"Yes."

"What did you think of it?"

"Nothing."

Eloquent response.

"I've given it a great deal of thought. And I've come to confirm what I wrote: if you try again, I won't stop you anymore."

Silence. I began again:

"I've thought it over: I understand you, Palamedes. Now I know that it's the only solution for you. I had a hard time accepting it, because it goes against what I've always been taught. You know how it is—life is the supreme value, respect for human life, and all that. . . . Thanks to you, I know that that's garbage: it depends on the person, like anything else on earth. And life doesn't agree with you, it's clear. I swear to you that I'm mad at myself: I regret having pulled you out of the garage."

A thousand tons of silence.

"I can imagine that a second attempt must seem daunting. And yet, as strange as it may seem, I've come to encourage you. That's right, Palamedes. I know that such an act demands a force of spirit of which I would be incapable: but I love life, so it's different. In your case, I urge you to find that determination."

Without noticing it, I had begun speaking with passion: I was getting carried away like Cicero, pronouncing the first diatribe against Catalina.

"Imagine in particular what will happen if you don't do it. You can't go on like this. Look at your existence: it's not a life! You're a mass of suffering and boredom. Worse than that: you're the void. And the void suffers, we know that since Bernanos. Of course, you haven't read him, you never read, in fact you never do anything. You are nothing, and you've probably never been anything. It wouldn't bother me if you were alone, but that's not the case: you take revenge for your fate on your wife, who, even if she doesn't look like a woman, is a thousand times more human than you are. You sequester her, you want to shape her into your void. It's despicable. If you're unable to live without oppressing someone, it's better not to live."

I was beginning to feel pretty good. The art of oratory was filling me with fire.

"What are you planning to do today, Palamedes? I'll describe your day for you: after you put away your groceries, you'll collapse into your armchair and watch four clocks until lunch. You'll prepare some rotten food, you'll gorge Bernadette on it and then gorge yourself, even though you hate eating, and particularly such disgusting food. Then you'll collapse again into the chair and watch the time pass, you'll watch the large and small hands move. Another meal-time ordeal, then you'll go to bed, and it will be the worst moment of your day: I suspect that you're an insomniac like me, and if my nights of insomnia are bad, what must yours be like? The insomnia of a fat pig who's bored and doesn't even hope to sleep since he doesn't like it. Because you don't like anything, Palamedes Bernardin! When you don't like anything, you have to die. You can't tell me that you don't have some pills that could help you in your medicine bag. It would be easier than the exhaust fumes. Courage, Palamedes! All you have to do is open your mouth, swallow a bottle of pills with a glass of water, go to bed, and it'll all be over—the boredom, the emptiness, the hassling with food, the clocks, your wife, and your insomnia! It will all be over, and you won't be here anymore to realize it. It will be salvation, Palamedes, salvation! For eternity!"

My cheeks were burning.

A monstrous thing happened that I wouldn't have thought possible: my neighbor began to laugh. We each have our own style of mirth: his was mean and weak, but all the more atrocious. It was as if he had internalized Parkinson's disease: you could see his intestines trembling as a procession of little cries emerged from his mouth.

It was a disgusting sight. What's more, he was looking me in the eyes. Vanquished, humiliated, nauseated, I went home.

That night, my plan took shape.

Mr. Bernardin possessed laughter. Some would therefore have concluded that he was a man, others that he was the devil.

But for my part, I wondered particularly about the significance of this laughter. Had he found my sermon comical? That would have suggested that he was a man of taste: a hypothesis I simply could not accept as true.

No, it must have been ironic laughter. I interpreted it as follows: "You'd like me to commit suicide, wouldn't you? You'd stop feeling guilty. Everything you just said is true, but you made me blow my only chance to leave this shitty life behind. No, it's not easy, even with pills. It took me seventy years to get up the courage. It would take me seventy more years to have the courage to try again. It's even harder when you know what it's like. And you—the one who botched my escape, who ruined my hope—you have the nerve to come and tell me these things! You're not even embarrassed! Well, my friend, if you really want me to die, kill me. If you want to redeem yourself, there's no other way: kill me!"

.   .   .

People are so wrong about the language of flowers. From then on, I understood the cry of the wisteria. Everything about it was supplication; its manner of attaching itself to the wall as if clinging to the dress of a queen, of letting its blue bunches fall like tearful lamentations. I could hear its menacing prayer: "Life is one long sorrow, an endless torture from which you could free me."

.   .   .

None of the objections I presented to myself held up: there was not the slightest reason for him to live, there was not the slightest reason for him not to die, I had not the slightest excuse not to kill him.

I chose the date of the summer solstice: it was a bit of a tacky resolution, but I was so lacking in courage that I needed to create a certain solemnity. Ceremony has always served to fortify the mind.

This decision calmed me down, or rather, the shift in the nature of my anxiety felt like a kind of remission.

I would execute my plan at night, since Emile Hazel by night was both more somber and more powerful. I said nothing to Juliette.

.   .   .

I waited until there was no trace of light in the sky. My wife was sleeping with her fists clenched. I crossed the bridge. The doors to the neighbors' house were all locked. I broke the garage window with my elbow, just as I did when I had thought I was saving Mr. Bernardin.

I went up to the second floor and entered the junk room that served as a bedroom to my tormenter. His bed seemed a shrine to discomfort. It was dark, but I could see like a cat: I immediately distinguished the fat man lying there, his eyes open. I had been right to think he was an insomniac.

For the first time, he didn't look at me with discontent. From the depths of his indifference rose a kind of relief: he knew why I had come.

He said nothing, and I said nothing; this was not a performance. As a messenger of the great Lady Death, I took up not a scythe but a pillow. I committed my act of mercy.

No one can imagine how easy it was.

. . .

When an obese, seventy-year old man dies in his bed, no one asks any questions.

I asked the police whether Juliette and I could assume responsibility for the wife of the defunct: there was no objection. They even told us what good people we were.

At the funeral, Bernadette made a very presentable widow.

. . .

Nothing is slower than hospital bills. At the end of September the statement arrived for the care Palamedes had received in early April, following his suicide attempt. I was the one who had written my name on the administrative forms and who had signed them; I was therefore being asked to settle the account.

I paid with a smile. It seemed fair: if I hadn't been stupid enough to drag him from the garage, after all, there wouldn't have been any hospital bills.

Moreover, since his death, I felt great friendship for my neighbor. It's a well-known syndrome: you love the people you help. On the night of April 2, I thought I had saved the life of Mr. Bernardin. How wrong I was—what an arrogant mistake!

On the other hand, on June 21, I didn't make a great show of myself, I didn't judge the fate of another by my own criteria, I didn't perform an act that would earn me the esteem of normal people; on the contrary, I had gone against my own nature, I had put the salvation of my neighbor before my own, with no chance of being commended by my peers. I had trampled my convictions, which were of little import, but also my inherent passivity, which was considerable, to fulfill the desire of a poor man—so that his wish would be granted, and not mine.

Ultimately, I had behaved in a generous manner: true generosity is that which cannot be understood. Once goodness becomes admirable, it is no longer goodness.

For it was during the night of the solstice that, in

the deepest sense of the expression, I saved the life of Palamedes Bernardin.

.   .   .

Juliette knows nothing. I shall never tell her. If she suspected that the man who shared her bed was a murderer, she would die of horror.

Thanks to her ignorance, she considered the death of our neighbor to be a good thing: she would finally be able to care for Bernadette. The Bernardin home became bright, clean, and airy. Every day my wife spends at least two hours with the cyst. She brings her cooked meals, flowers, and picture books. She often invites me to accompany her; I refuse, because the idea of witnessing Bernadette's bath sends chills down my spine.

"She's my best friend," Juliette told me after several months.

The countess of Ségur would have cried tears of emotion.

.   .   .

Today it is snowing, just like a year ago, upon our arrival here. I watch as the flakes fall. "When the snow melts, where does the whiteness go?" asked Prétextat Tach. It seems to me there is no greater question.

My whiteness has melted, and no one has noticed. When

I moved into the House, twelve months ago, I knew who I was: an obscure Greek and Latin teacher whose life would leave no trace.

Now I watch the snow. It too will melt without a trace. But I understand, now, that it is a mystery.

I no longer know anything about myself.

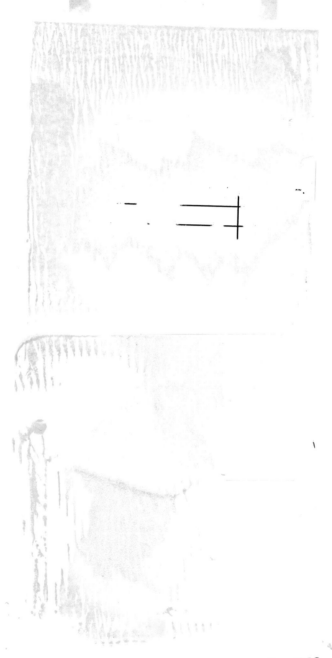

JAN 3 1 1998